TABLE OF

CHAPTER 1
Prologue: Shadows of the Heart

CHAPTER 2
The Weight of Expectation

CHAPTER 3
Love in the Shadows

CHAPTER 4
A Deal Sealed in Blood

CHAPTER 5
A Forbidden Goodbye

CHAPTER 6
Wedding Bells or Chains?

CHAPTER 7
Betrayal & Consequences

CHAPTER 8
Exile & Survival

CHAPTER 9
Shadows of the Past

CHAPTER 10
A Mother's Plea

CHAPTER 11
A Family Divided

CHAPTER 12
The Test of Forgiveness

CHAPTER 13
Redemption & New Beginnings

© 2025 Zula Tlholoe. All rights reserved.
No part of this book may be reproduced, stored in a retrieval system, or transmitted in any form or by any means, whether electronic, mechanical, photocopying, recording, or otherwise, without the prior written permission of the publisher or author, except for brief quotations used in critical reviews or other non-commercial uses permitted by copyright law.

First Edition, 2025
Published by: Zula Tlholoe
Cover design by: Zula Tlholoe
ISBN: 9798314953730

Disclaimer:
The characters, events, and situations depicted in this book are entirely fictional. Any resemblance to actual persons, living or dead, is purely coincidental. The author and publisher make no representations or warranties with respect to the accuracy, completeness, or usefulness of the information contained in this book

CHAPTER: 1

PROLOGUE: SHADOWS OF THE HEART

The air hung thick and heavy, laden with the scent of jasmine and the rhythmic pulse of drums echoing from the village square. Amina sat upon a low stool, her posture ramrod straight, her hands clasped tightly in her lap. The vibrant colors of her traditional attire – a deep indigo wrapper adorned with intricate gold embroidery – felt like a suffocating weight rather than a celebration. Today was her betrothal ceremony, a day that should have been filled with joy and anticipation, a day that marked the beginning of her journey into womanhood and the promise of a future filled with love and companionship.

But for Amina, the joy was a hollow echo, the anticipation a gnawing dread. Her heart felt like a trapped bird, beating frantically against the confines of her chest, desperate for escape. The man she was to be betrothed to, Kwame, was a man of stature and respect within their community. He was kind, diligent, and came from a family of considerable influence. He was, by all accounts, a suitable match, a man any young woman in the village would be fortunate to marry. Yet, Amina's heart remained stubbornly unmoved.

Kwame represented everything that was expected of her – duty, obedience, and the continuation of tradition. He was a symbol of the life that had been carefully mapped out for her since birth, a life where her choices were dictated by the needs of her family and the customs of her ancestors. He was a good man, she knew, but he was not *her* man. He did not ignite the spark within her soul, the yearning for connection that whispered in her dreams.

Her gaze drifted towards the entrance of the courtyard, her heart quickening its pace. She knew he wouldn't be there, not officially. His presence would be a blatant act of defiance, a challenge to the established order that would bring shame and dishonor upon her family. But still, she couldn't help but search for him, to hope for a glimpse, a fleeting moment of connection that would remind her that she wasn't entirely alone in her despair.

Kwame was a man molded by the traditions of the village, a man who respected the elders and adhered to the customs passed down through generations. He was a pillar of the community, a symbol of stability and continuity. He represented the old ways, the established order, the unwavering belief in the wisdom of the ancestors. He was everything Amina's family wanted for her, everything the village expected her to be.

The drums beat louder, the chanting grew more fervent, and Amina felt the weight of expectation pressing down upon her, threatening to crush her spirit. She was a pawn in a game she didn't understand, a sacrifice on the altar of tradition. Her future was not her own, her choices had been made for her, and her voice was silenced by the deafening roar of societal pressure.

She knew that her family loved her, that they believed they were acting in her best interest. They saw Kwame as a provider, a protector, a man who could offer her security and stability. They couldn't understand the longing in her heart, the yearning for something more than a comfortable existence. They couldn't comprehend the idea that love, true love, was more important than social standing or financial security.

Amina closed her eyes, a single tear escaping and tracing a path down her cheek. She prayed for strength, for guidance, for a way out of this impossible situation. She prayed for a miracle, a sign that would show her the right path to take. But the silence within her heart was deafening, broken only by the relentless rhythm of the drums, a constant reminder of the fate that awaited her.

The women of her family fussed around her, adjusting her veil, smoothing her dress, whispering words of encouragement and advice. They saw her as a lucky girl, a fortunate bride, a woman on the cusp of a blessed future. They couldn't see the turmoil raging within her, the silent battle between duty and desire, the agonizing choice she was being forced to make.

Her heart ached with a longing that threatened to consume her. She yearned for a life filled with passion, with laughter, with the freedom to choose her own destiny. She dreamed of a love that was not dictated by tradition or societal expectations, a love that was born of mutual respect, understanding, and a deep connection of souls. But that dream seemed impossibly distant, a shimmering mirage in the vast desert of her predetermined future.

The air hung thick with the scent of incense and anticipation. Amina sat upon a low stool, her posture as rigid as the starched linen of her traditional attire. Around her, the courtyard buzzed with activity – women gossiping in hushed tones, children darting between legs like playful spirits, and men conferring with serious expressions, their voices a low rumble that vibrated through the very ground beneath her feet. Today was her betrothal ceremony, a day that should have been filled with joy and celebration. Yet, a knot of dread tightened in her stomach with each passing moment.

Kwame, the man chosen for her, was a figure of respect within their community. He was strong, dependable, and came from a family of considerable influence. A match with him would undoubtedly secure her family's standing, solidifying their place within the intricate tapestry of village life. Everyone told her how fortunate she was, how blessed to have been chosen by such a man. But their words felt hollow, echoing in the vast emptiness that had taken root in her heart.

Amina glanced down at the intricate henna patterns adorning her hands, the swirling designs a stark contrast to the turmoil raging within her. Each stroke represented a blessing, a wish for prosperity and fertility in her marriage. But what good were blessings when they were bestowed upon a union devoid of love? What good was prosperity when it came at the cost of her own happiness?

She longed for a different life, a life where love was not a transaction, where her heart dictated her path, not the expectations of her family. But such desires were considered frivolous, even selfish, in their village. Tradition was the bedrock upon which their society was built, and to deviate from it was to invite chaos and dishonor.

As the drums began to beat, signaling the start of the ceremony, Amina's heart pounded in her chest like a trapped bird. She knew what was expected of her: a demure smile, a graceful curtsy, and a silent acceptance of the fate that had been laid out before her. But as she raised her head, her gaze collided with another across the crowded courtyard.

Malik. He stood in the shadows, a figure of quiet intensity amidst the vibrant chaos. His eyes, dark and knowing, met hers with a force that stole her breath away. In that fleeting moment, the world around her seemed to fade into a blur, the drums silenced, the voices muted. There was only him, and the unspoken promise that shimmered between them.

Malik was everything Kwame was not. He was an outsider, a man who had carved his own path through sheer determination and grit. He possessed a rebellious spirit, a refusal to conform to the rigid expectations of their society. And he loved her, with a fierce and unwavering passion that mirrored her own.

Their love was a secret, a dangerous flame that they had carefully guarded in the shadows. It was a love born of stolen glances, whispered conversations under the cloak of darkness, and shared dreams of a life beyond the confines of their village. It was a love that defied tradition, challenged expectations, and threatened to shatter the very foundation of Amina's world.

The drums beat louder, pulling Amina back to the present. She knew that this stolen moment, this forbidden connection, was a dangerous game. If their secret were to be discovered, the consequences would be devastating. Shame would be brought upon her family, and she would be ostracized, cast out from the only community she had ever known.

Yet, as she gazed into Malik's eyes, she knew that she could not deny the truth that burned within her. Her heart belonged to him, and to surrender to a loveless marriage would be to betray not only herself but also the very essence of her being. The choice before her was impossible, a cruel twist of fate that pitted love against duty, desire against tradition.

In that single, stolen glance, the central conflict of Amina's life was ignited. It was a battle between the expectations of her family and the desires of her heart, between the traditions of her village and the yearning for personal freedom. It was a conflict that would test her faith, challenge her courage, and ultimately determine the course of her destiny.

The shadows deepened around Malik, obscuring his features, but Amina could still feel the weight of his gaze upon her. It was a silent plea, a desperate hope that she would choose love over obligation. But as the ceremony began in earnest, Amina knew that the path ahead would be fraught with peril, and that the price of love might be higher than she could ever imagine.

The village of Naledi, nestled deep within the heartland, was a place where time seemed to move at a different pace. Generations had lived and died within its embrace, their lives intertwined with the rhythms of the land and the unwavering adherence to ancestral customs. The air itself hummed with the weight of tradition, a palpable presence that shaped every aspect of daily life, from the clothes people wore to the songs they sang.

Faith, both in the Christian God and in the spirits of their ancestors, was the bedrock upon which Naledi was built. The small, whitewashed church at the center of the village was a testament to their devotion, its bell tolling each Sunday, calling the faithful to prayer. Yet, alongside the hymns and sermons, ancient rituals persisted, whispered blessings and offerings made in the sacred grove on the outskirts of town, a place where the veil between the living and the dead seemed thin.

Family honor was the lifeblood of Naledi, a currency more valuable than gold. Every action, every decision, was weighed against its potential impact on the family's reputation. Marriages were not merely unions of two individuals but strategic alliances, carefully orchestrated to strengthen bonds, consolidate power, and ensure the continuation of the family line. Love, while not entirely absent, was often considered a secondary concern, a pleasant addition if it happened to blossom, but never the primary foundation upon which a marriage was built.

Amina had grown up within this intricate web of tradition, faith, and family honor. She knew the expectations placed upon her, the path that had been laid out for her since birth. She had always been a dutiful daughter, respectful of her elders, and compliant with their wishes. But beneath the surface of obedience, a quiet rebellion stirred, a yearning for something more than what tradition dictated.

The houses in Naledi were built close together, their walls almost touching, symbolizing the interconnectedness of the community. Smoke curled from the chimneys in the early mornings, carrying the scent of woodsmoke and cooking fires, a comforting aroma that spoke of shared meals and communal gatherings. The marketplace was the heart of the village, a vibrant hub of activity where farmers sold their produce, artisans displayed their crafts, and neighbors exchanged news and gossip.

The elders of Naledi, the keepers of tradition, held immense power. Their words carried weight, their decisions were rarely questioned, and their influence extended to every corner of the village. They were the guardians of the past, determined to preserve the customs and beliefs that had sustained their community for generations. Mansa, Amina's grandfather, was among the most respected and influential of these elders, his word law within their family.

But even in Naledi, change was beginning to stir. The younger generation, exposed to the outside world through education and travel, were starting to question the old ways. They saw the allure of modernity, the promise of individual freedom, and the possibility of a life unburdened by the weight of tradition. This growing tension between the old and the new threatened to unravel the very fabric of Naledi society.

Amina found herself caught in the middle of this generational divide. She respected her elders and valued her family, but she also yearned for the freedom to choose her own path, to love whom she pleased, and to define her own destiny. The conflict within her grew stronger with each passing day, threatening to tear her apart.

The river that flowed through Naledi was more than just a source of water; it was a symbol of life, a constant reminder of the cyclical nature of existence. Women gathered at its banks to wash clothes, children played in its shallows, and lovers met in secret beneath the shade of the willow trees that lined its banks. It was a place of both joy and sorrow, a witness to the triumphs and tragedies of the village.

As Amina sat adorned in traditional attire, awaiting her betrothal ceremony, she felt the weight of Naledi's traditions pressing down upon her. The village, with its unwavering faith and its unyielding adherence to family honor, seemed to hold her captive, a prisoner of its ancient customs. But within her heart, a flicker of hope remained, a belief that even in Naledi, love could find a way to triumph over tradition.

Amina's heart was a battlefield, a relentless clash between the ironclad walls of duty and the untamed wilderness of her own desires. The weight of her family's expectations pressed down on her, a heavy cloak woven from generations of tradition. She had been raised to understand her place, to accept the path laid out for her with grace and obedience. Marriage was not a matter of personal inclination but a sacred pact, a binding agreement that strengthened the bonds of family and community. Kwame was a suitable match, a man of standing and influence, whose union with Amina would elevate her family's status. This was the narrative she had always known, the script she was expected to follow without question.

Yet, within the depths of her soul, a different story was unfolding. It was a story whispered by stolen glances, fueled by secret rendezvous, and etched onto her heart by the undeniable presence of Malik. He was everything her family was not: an outsider, a challenger to the established order, a man who dared to dream beyond the confines of tradition. His eyes held a fire that mirrored her own yearning for freedom, his words a melody that resonated with her deepest desires. With him, Amina felt alive, seen, and understood in a way that no arranged marriage could ever offer.

The conflict raged within her, a tempestuous storm that threatened to tear her apart. Each beat of her heart was a drumbeat of war, a constant reminder of the impossible choice she faced. To choose Kwame was to betray her own soul, to suffocate the flame of love that burned within her. It was to resign herself to a life of quiet desperation, a gilded cage where duty reigned supreme and personal happiness was a forgotten dream. But to choose Malik was to defy her family, to shatter the foundations of her community, and to risk exile and shame. It was to become an outcast, a pariah, forever branded as the woman who dared to challenge tradition.

As the betrothal ceremony drew nearer, the pressure mounted, squeezing the air from her lungs and tightening the knot in her stomach. Every smile from her mother, every word of encouragement from her father, felt like a hammer blow to her heart. They saw her as a dutiful daughter, a vessel of family honor, blissfully unaware of the turmoil that consumed her. How could she explain to them the depth of her love for Malik, the soul-deep connection that transcended social boundaries and cultural expectations? How could she make them understand that her happiness was not a commodity to be bartered, but a fundamental right to be cherished?

Sleep offered no respite, only a relentless replay of the agonizing dilemma. In her dreams, she saw herself walking down two separate paths. One was paved with gold, lined with smiling faces, and adorned with the trappings of wealth and status. But as she walked, the path grew colder, the smiles faded, and the gold turned to dust. The other path was shrouded in shadows, fraught with peril, and marked by the thorns of societal disapproval. But as she walked, a warm hand reached for hers, a familiar voice whispered words of love and encouragement, and the darkness began to dissipate, revealing a glimmer of hope.

The weight of her decision threatened to crush her, to extinguish the very spark of life within her. She sought solace in prayer, pouring out her heart to God, begging for guidance and strength. Was it her duty to sacrifice her own happiness for the sake of her family? Or was it her right to follow the path that her heart had chosen, even if it meant defying tradition and risking everything she held dear? The answer remained elusive, shrouded in a veil of uncertainty.

She found herself wandering to the riverbank, the gentle murmur of the water a soothing balm to her troubled soul. The river, a symbol of life and renewal, had always been a place of reflection for her. As she gazed into its depths, she saw her own reflection staring back, a face etched with worry and uncertainty. Was she strong enough to defy tradition? Was she brave enough to risk everything for love? The questions echoed in her mind, unanswered, unresolved.

The faces of her family swam before her eyes – her mother, with her gentle smile and unwavering faith; her father, with his stern demeanor and deep-seated sense of honor; her grandmother, with her wise eyes and gentle touch. How could she bear to disappoint them, to shatter their dreams for her future? But then she saw Malik's face, his eyes filled with love and hope, his hand outstretched, beckoning her to join him on a journey of self-discovery and shared happiness. The choice was hers, and hers alone.

As the sun began to set, casting long shadows across the village, Amina knew that she could no longer remain silent. She could no longer suppress the voice of her heart, the yearning for freedom, the undeniable love that bound her to Malik. The time had come to make a decision, to choose her own destiny, to embrace the path that lay before her, no matter the cost. The battle within her was far from over, but a sense of resolve had begun to take root, a quiet determination to fight for her own happiness, even if it meant challenging the very foundations of her world.

Amina knew that the path ahead would be fraught with challenges, with heartbreak, and with uncertainty. But she also knew that she could not live a lie, that she could not deny the truth that burned within her soul. She would face her family, she would face her community, and she would face the consequences of her actions with courage and grace. For she knew, deep down, that love was worth fighting for, that freedom was worth risking everything for, and that her own happiness was not a selfish desire, but a sacred right.

Amina's heart fluttered, a trapped bird against the confines of her ribs. The vibrant colors of her traditional attire felt like a suffocating shroud, each thread a testament to the expectations that bound her. The intricate patterns, passed down through generations, seemed to whisper tales of duty and sacrifice, tales that echoed in the rhythmic beating of the drums that signaled the start of the betrothal ceremony. She knew what was expected of her – a graceful acceptance of Kwame, a man chosen for her, a man who represented security and the continuation of her family's legacy. But her gaze kept drifting towards the shadows, towards the one face that ignited a fire within her, a fire that threatened to consume the very foundations of her carefully constructed world.

Malik. His name was a prayer and a curse on her lips, a melody that haunted her waking hours and a forbidden desire that danced in her dreams. He stood apart, an outsider in his own village, his eyes mirroring the turmoil that raged within her. Their stolen glances, brief and fleeting, were a language of their own, a silent conversation that spoke of longing and a love that defied the boundaries of tradition. Each stolen moment was a rebellion, a dangerous game that could shatter everything she held dear. But the risk, the potential for ruin, was a siren's call she couldn't resist.

The air crackled with unspoken tension, a heavy weight that pressed down on Amina's shoulders. She knew that her family, her community, would never understand her feelings for Malik. He was not of their world, not of their choosing. He was a threat to the established order, a disruption to the carefully woven tapestry of their lives. To choose him would be to betray her family, to bring shame upon their name, to become an outcast in the very place she called home.

Yet, the thought of a life without Malik was a desolate landscape, a barren wasteland devoid of color and joy. To marry Kwame would be to suffocate her soul, to imprison her heart in a gilded cage. It would be a life of quiet desperation, a slow and agonizing death of her spirit. The choice was a cruel paradox, a Sophie's Choice of the heart, where both options led to unimaginable pain.

As the drums beat louder, as the ceremony drew closer, Amina felt a sense of dread wash over her. The weight of her impossible situation threatened to crush her, to suffocate the very life out of her. She knew that the path ahead was fraught with peril, a treacherous journey through a minefield of expectations and societal pressures. The whispers of doubt grew louder in her mind, questioning her strength, her resolve, her ability to withstand the storm that was brewing on the horizon.

The fleeting joy of stolen moments with Malik would soon be replaced by the harsh reality of her arranged marriage. The warmth of his touch would fade into the cold indifference of a loveless union. The dreams they shared would become distant memories, replaced by the suffocating routine of a life chosen for her, not by her. The vibrant colors of her world would slowly fade into a monotonous gray, a reflection of the emptiness that would consume her soul.

But amidst the despair, a flicker of defiance ignited within her. A spark of hope, however small, refused to be extinguished. She knew that she was not alone in her struggle. Other women in her village had faced similar choices, had sacrificed their own happiness for the sake of family honor. But Amina refused to become another silent victim, another forgotten soul lost in the annals of tradition.

She would find a way, she vowed, to navigate this impossible situation, to find a path that honored both her family and her heart. It would not be easy, she knew, but she was not one to back down from a challenge. The fire that burned within her, the love that defied boundaries, would guide her through the darkness, would give her the strength to face whatever lay ahead.

Yet, even as she made this silent vow, a sense of foreboding lingered. The shadows of the heart were long and deep, and the path to happiness was often paved with heartbreak and sacrifice. Amina knew that the journey ahead would test her faith, her courage, and her very soul. But she was ready, or so she hoped, to face whatever challenges lay ahead, for the sake of love, for the sake of her own freedom.

The prologue served as a stark reminder that Amina's story was not a fairy tale, but a reflection of the complex realities faced by many women in her community. It was a story of love and loss, of duty and defiance, of faith and fire. And as the drums continued to beat, as the ceremony drew ever closer, Amina braced herself for the storm that was about to break, knowing that her life would never be the same again.

CHAPTER: 2

THE WEIGHT OF EXPECTATION

The air in the village of Naledi hummed with anticipation. Amina's upcoming marriage to Kwame was not merely a union of two individuals; it was a strategic alliance, a carefully orchestrated move that promised to elevate her family's standing within the community. Her parents, especially her mother, Thandiwe, beamed with pride whenever the topic was broached. They saw it as a testament to their unwavering adherence to tradition, a validation of their efforts to instill in Amina the values they held so dear: respect, obedience, and a deep understanding of her role in preserving their heritage.

For the Mokoena family, Amina's marriage to Kwame represented more than just personal happiness; it was a crucial step in solidifying their position among the village elite. Kwame's family, the Dlamini's, were known for their wealth and influence, their sprawling farmlands a testament to generations of hard work and shrewd decision-making. A union between the two families would not only bring economic prosperity but also enhance their social capital, opening doors to new opportunities and solidifying their place at the heart of Naledi's intricate social web.

Thandiwe, in particular, saw this marriage as the culmination of her lifelong aspirations for Amina. She had always envisioned a future for her daughter that was rooted in tradition, a future where she would uphold the values of their ancestors and contribute to the continued prosperity of their family. Kwame, with his strong ties to the community and his unwavering commitment to upholding their customs, seemed like the perfect embodiment of that vision. He was a man of substance, a man of integrity, and a man who would undoubtedly provide Amina with a secure and comfortable life.

The whispers of admiration and envy followed Amina wherever she went. The women of the village, their eyes gleaming with a mixture of awe and longing, would often stop her to offer their congratulations, their voices laced with a hint of wistful resignation. They spoke of Kwame's virtues, his generosity, his unwavering loyalty to his family, and his undeniable charm. Amina would nod politely, offering a demure smile in return, but beneath the surface, a storm of conflicting emotions raged within her.

The preparations for the wedding were elaborate and meticulously planned. The Mokoena homestead was abuzz with activity, as relatives from far and wide descended upon Naledi to partake in the festivities. The women of the family, their hands stained with henna, worked tirelessly to prepare the traditional delicacies that would be served at the ceremony. The men, their voices booming with laughter and camaraderie, gathered to discuss the logistics of the event, ensuring that every detail was executed flawlessly.

Amina found herself caught in a whirlwind of expectations, her every move scrutinized, her every word carefully weighed. She was the center of attention, the star of this grand production, but she felt like a mere puppet, her strings being pulled by forces beyond her control. The weight of her family's pride, the pressure to conform to tradition, and the gnawing uncertainty about her own future threatened to suffocate her.

Even Mansa, her usually stoic grandfather, seemed to soften in her presence, his eyes twinkling with a rare display of affection. He would often call her aside, his voice raspy with age, to impart words of wisdom and encouragement. He spoke of the importance of family, the sanctity of marriage, and the enduring power of tradition. Amina would listen attentively, absorbing his words like a sponge, but deep down, a part of her yearned for something more, something that transcended the boundaries of duty and obligation.

The village elders, too, played their part in reinforcing the significance of Amina's union. They saw it as a symbol of continuity, a reaffirmation of their commitment to preserving the cultural heritage of Naledi. They spoke of the importance of arranged marriages in maintaining social order, ensuring the stability of the community, and preventing the erosion of their traditions in the face of modernization.

As the wedding day drew nearer, Amina found herself increasingly isolated, trapped in a gilded cage of expectations. The smiles and congratulations of her family and friends felt like a constant reminder of the sacrifice she was expected to make, the dreams she was expected to relinquish. The weight of their pride, their hopes, and their aspirations pressed down on her, threatening to crush her spirit.

Yet, amidst the whirlwind of preparations and the chorus of expectations, a small flicker of defiance began to ignite within Amina's heart. A whisper of doubt, a seed of rebellion, began to take root, challenging the very foundations of her obedience and threatening to unravel the carefully constructed facade of her compliance. The path ahead was fraught with uncertainty, but Amina knew, deep down, that she could no longer ignore the voice within her, the voice that yearned for a love that was not dictated by tradition, a future that was not predetermined by duty.

The day of the pre-marriage ceremony dawned with an oppressive weight of expectation. Amina moved through the rituals like a ghost, her heart a leaden weight in her chest. The vibrant colors of her traditional attire felt like a costume, a disguise that hid the turmoil within. Family members bustled around her, their faces beaming with pride and anticipation. They saw this union as a strategic alliance, a way to solidify their family's standing within the community. Her mother, usually a source of comfort, now seemed distant, her eyes reflecting a steely resolve that brooked no argument.

Amina understood the importance of family. It was the bedrock of their society, the source of their strength and identity. But what about her own happiness? Was she simply a pawn in a game of power and prestige? The thought gnawed at her, a persistent whisper that threatened to unravel the carefully constructed façade of obedience.

Later that evening, as the celebrations wound down, Amina found herself seeking refuge in the cool shadows of the courtyard. The air was thick with the scent of jasmine and woodsmoke, a familiar fragrance that usually brought her solace. But tonight, it only amplified her sense of unease. She longed for a moment of peace, a chance to escape the suffocating expectations that surrounded her.

It was then that Jabulani, her uncle, approached. Unlike the other members of her family, Jabulani had traveled extensively, exposing him to different cultures and perspectives. He possessed a quiet wisdom, a gentle understanding that set him apart. Amina had always felt a kinship with him, a sense that he saw beyond the surface, recognizing the complexities that lay beneath.

Jabulani sat beside her on the stone bench, his gaze thoughtful. He didn't speak immediately, allowing the silence to settle between them. Amina knew that he sensed her distress, that he understood the burden she carried.

"Amina," he began, his voice soft but firm, "you look troubled. This marriage... it is a great honor, of course. Kwame is a good man, from a respected family."

Amina nodded, acknowledging the truth in his words. Kwame was indeed a good man. He was kind, responsible, and respected within the community. But he wasn't Malik. He didn't ignite a fire in her soul, didn't make her heart soar with a joy that defied explanation.

Jabulani paused, his eyes searching hers. "But is it what *you* want, Amina? Is it what will truly make you happy?"

His words hung in the air, heavy with unspoken meaning. Amina's heart skipped a beat. No one had ever dared to ask her that question so directly. It was a question that she had been afraid to ask herself, a question that threatened to shatter the foundations of her carefully constructed world.

"A marriage without love," Jabulani continued, his voice barely a whisper, "is a house without a foundation. It may stand for a time, but eventually, it will crumble."

His words struck Amina like a thunderbolt, illuminating the darkness within her. She had always known, deep down, that something was missing, that this marriage was not the path her heart desired. But she had suppressed those feelings, burying them beneath layers of duty and obligation. Jabulani's words gave her permission to acknowledge the truth, to confront the reality of her situation.

Amina looked at her uncle, her eyes filled with a mixture of gratitude and fear. He had planted a seed of doubt in her mind, a seed that threatened to blossom into rebellion. But he had also offered her a glimmer of hope, a possibility that she could choose her own destiny.

"I... I don't know, Uncle," she stammered, her voice trembling. "I want to do what is right, what is best for my family. But... but I also want to be happy."

Jabulani smiled gently, his eyes filled with compassion. "Happiness is not a selfish desire, Amina. It is a gift, a blessing from God. And you deserve to be happy."

He squeezed her hand reassuringly, then rose to his feet. "Think about what I have said, Amina. Pray about it. And trust your heart. It will guide you."

With that, he turned and walked away, leaving Amina alone in the shadows. His words echoed in her mind, a constant reminder of the choice that lay before her. The weight of expectation had suddenly become unbearable, crushing her beneath its immense pressure. But within that weight, a tiny spark of defiance had been ignited, a flicker of hope that refused to be extinguished.

The weight of expectation settled upon Amina like a heavy cloak, stifling her spirit and dimming the light in her eyes. Everywhere she turned, she was met with the unwavering gaze of her elders, their faces etched with the unspoken command to uphold tradition. The village, nestled in the heart of the fertile valley, seemed to hum with the collective will of generations past, their voices echoing in the rustling leaves and the gentle flow of the river. Amina felt herself caught in a current, swept along by forces beyond her control, her own desires and dreams fading into the background.

The whispers followed her like shadows, clinging to her every step. "Amina is so fortunate," they would say, their voices laced with envy and admiration. "Kwame is a fine man, from a respected family. This marriage will bring great honor to your lineage." But what about her own happiness? What about the quiet longings of her heart, the dreams that fluttered within her like caged birds? These questions remained unspoken, trapped within the confines of her own mind, for to voice them would be to invite disapproval, to shatter the carefully constructed facade of obedience and conformity.

The societal pressure was relentless, a constant reminder of her duty to her family and her community. From the youngest child to the oldest elder, everyone seemed to have an opinion on her impending marriage. The women, gathered around the communal fire, would share stories of their own arranged unions, tales of sacrifice and resilience, of finding love and contentment within the boundaries of tradition. But Amina couldn't shake the feeling that something was missing, that there was a deeper, more profound connection to be found, a love that transcended duty and obligation.

She thought of her mother, a woman who had dutifully accepted her own arranged marriage, raising a family and upholding the values of their community. Amina loved her mother dearly, but she couldn't help but wonder if there was a flicker of regret hidden beneath her placid smile, a yearning for a life unlived. Was she destined to follow the same path, to sacrifice her own happiness for the sake of tradition? The thought sent a shiver down her spine, a cold premonition of a future devoid of passion and joy.

Even the village elders, with their weathered faces and their pronouncements of wisdom, seemed to reinforce the importance of conformity. They spoke of the dangers of straying from the path of tradition, of the chaos and disruption that could ensue if individuals were allowed to follow their own desires. Amina listened respectfully, but her heart remained unconvinced. She couldn't reconcile the idea of a loving God with the notion of a life devoid of personal choice, a future dictated by the expectations of others.

The weight of it all threatened to crush her, to extinguish the flame of hope that still flickered within her breast. She longed to confide in someone, to share the burden of her doubts and fears, but she knew that to do so would be to invite criticism and condemnation. Her parents, though loving, were staunch believers in tradition, and her friends, though sympathetic, were bound by the same societal constraints. She felt utterly alone, adrift in a sea of expectations, with no safe harbor in sight.

The vibrant colors of her traditional attire seemed to mock her, the intricate patterns a symbol of the intricate web of obligations that bound her. The rhythmic beat of the drums during the evening celebrations felt like a countdown, each beat bringing her closer to a future she didn't want, a life that wasn't truly her own. She yearned to break free, to escape the suffocating embrace of tradition, but the fear of disappointing her family and shaming her community held her captive.

As she walked through the village, she couldn't help but notice the subtle differences in the way she was now perceived. The villagers, once so warm and welcoming, now regarded her with a mixture of pity and expectation. They saw her as a bride-to-be, a symbol of their community's strength and continuity. They didn't see the turmoil raging within her, the silent battle between duty and desire. She was a vessel, an instrument of tradition, her own identity subsumed by the collective will of the village.

Even her dreams offered no respite, filled with images of a life unlived, of opportunities lost and passions unfulfilled. She saw herself trapped in a gilded cage, surrounded by comfort and security, but devoid of true happiness. She woke each morning with a sense of dread, the weight of expectation pressing down on her like a physical burden. The days stretched out before her, a monotonous procession of rituals and preparations, each one a step closer to the altar and a life she didn't choose.

Yet, amidst the darkness, a tiny spark of defiance flickered within her. The memory of Jabulani's words, "A marriage without love is a house without a foundation," echoed in her mind, a reminder that there was another way, a different path to be taken. And as she gazed out at the rolling hills and the endless sky, she couldn't shake the feeling that her destiny lay beyond the confines of tradition, that there was a greater purpose for her life, a love that was worth fighting for, even if it meant defying the expectations of her family and her community.

In the heart of the village, arranged marriages were not merely a tradition; they were the bedrock of social order, the invisible threads that wove together families, clans, and the very fabric of their community. These unions were seen as strategic alliances, carefully orchestrated to ensure the prosperity and stability of the village for generations to come. They were a testament to the belief that the collective good outweighed individual desires, a sacrifice made willingly for the greater harmony of all.

The elders, revered for their wisdom and experience, held the sacred responsibility of matchmaking. They meticulously assessed potential partners, considering factors far beyond mere attraction or affection. Lineage, wealth, social standing, and even the perceived temperament of the families involved were all weighed with utmost care. Their decisions were not taken lightly, for they understood that the fate of the village rested, in part, on the success of these unions.

For generations, this system had served the village well, fostering a sense of unity and shared purpose. Families were interconnected through marriage, creating a network of support and cooperation that strengthened the community as a whole. Disputes were often resolved through familial ties, and resources were shared among those who were bound by blood and marriage.

Amina, having grown up within this intricate web of tradition, understood the significance of arranged marriages. She had witnessed firsthand the benefits they brought to the village: the stability, the security, and the sense of belonging that came from being part of a larger, interconnected family. She knew that by accepting her arranged marriage to Kwame, she would be contributing to this legacy, upholding the traditions that had sustained her community for centuries.

However, as she sat at the pre-marriage ceremony, dressed in traditional attire and knowing that she was about to be betrothed to a man she did not love, a sense of unease began to creep into her heart. The weight of expectation pressed down on her, threatening to suffocate her spirit. She couldn't shake the feeling that something was amiss, that there was more to marriage than mere duty and obligation.

The whispers of doubt planted by her uncle Jabulani echoed in her mind. He had questioned the very foundation of arranged marriages, suggesting that love was an essential ingredient for a successful union. His words challenged the long-held beliefs of the village, forcing Amina to confront the possibility that tradition might not always be right.

As she looked around at the faces of her family and community, she saw the pride and expectation in their eyes. They believed that she was making the right choice, that she was fulfilling her duty and contributing to the greater good. But what about her own happiness? What about her own desires and dreams?

The cultural significance of arranged marriages extended beyond mere practicality; it was deeply intertwined with their spiritual beliefs. Marriage was seen as a sacred covenant, a bond that transcended the physical realm and connected families to their ancestors. It was a way of honoring the past and ensuring the continuation of their lineage.

The ancestors were believed to watch over the village, guiding their decisions and ensuring their prosperity. By upholding the tradition of arranged marriages, the villagers were paying homage to their ancestors and seeking their blessings. To defy this tradition would be seen as a sign of disrespect, a rejection of their heritage, and a betrayal of their ancestors' wishes.

Amina understood the weight of this responsibility, the burden of upholding the traditions that had been passed down for generations. She knew that her decision would not only affect her own life but also the lives of her family and community. The pressure to conform was immense, threatening to crush her spirit and extinguish the flame of her own desires.

Yet, as she glanced across the courtyard and saw Malik standing in the shadows, a flicker of hope ignited within her. His presence was a reminder that there was another way, a path that led to love and personal fulfillment. But could she dare to defy tradition, to risk everything for the sake of her own happiness? The answer, she knew, lay within her own heart.

The role of arranged marriages in maintaining social order was undeniable. They served as a mechanism for preserving the status quo, ensuring that power and wealth remained within the hands of established families. They also helped to prevent social unrest by minimizing the potential for conflicts arising from romantic relationships.

However, this system also had its drawbacks. It often stifled individual expression and limited the choices available to young people, particularly women. The emphasis on duty and obligation often overshadowed the importance of personal happiness, leading to a sense of resentment and dissatisfaction.

Amina found herself caught between these two opposing forces: the desire to uphold tradition and the yearning for personal freedom. She knew that her decision would have far-reaching consequences, not only for herself but also for her family and community. The weight of expectation was heavy, but she refused to let it crush her spirit. She would find a way to honor her family while also pursuing her own happiness, even if it meant defying the very foundations of their social order.

Kwame, a man of considerable standing within the village, was the embodiment of tradition and familial pride. His lineage was long and respected, his family having contributed significantly to the prosperity and stability of their community for generations. He carried himself with an air of quiet confidence, a demeanor cultivated from years of knowing his place in the world and understanding the expectations that came with it.

From Kwame's perspective, the arranged marriage with Amina was not merely a union of two individuals, but a strategic alliance between two prominent families. He saw it as a way to solidify their positions within the village, ensuring continued prosperity and influence for both households. He believed in the wisdom of his elders, trusting that their guidance would lead him and Amina down a path of mutual benefit and lasting harmony.

He envisioned a future with Amina that was rooted in tradition, respect, and shared values. He expected her to be a dutiful wife, a supportive partner, and a loving mother to their children. He anticipated that she would embrace her role within the family and community, upholding the customs and traditions that had been passed down for generations.

Kwame's expectations were not born out of malice or a desire to control Amina, but rather from a deep-seated belief in the importance of maintaining social order and preserving their cultural heritage. He saw himself as a protector and provider, responsible for ensuring Amina's well-being and the continuation of their family's legacy.

However, beneath Kwame's composed exterior lay a subtle sense of entitlement, a belief that Amina should be grateful for the opportunity to marry into his family. He viewed himself as a desirable match, a man of wealth, status, and unwavering commitment to tradition. He expected Amina to recognize the value of this union and to embrace her role with enthusiasm and gratitude.

The power dynamics at play were undeniable. Kwame held a position of authority within the relationship, not only due to his gender but also because of his family's influence and his adherence to traditional values. He expected Amina to defer to his judgment, to respect his decisions, and to prioritize the needs of the family above her own desires.

He had observed other marriages within the village, noting the wives who dutifully served their husbands and families, earning respect and admiration within the community. He anticipated that Amina would follow a similar path, finding fulfillment in her role as a wife and mother, and contributing to the overall well-being of their household.

Kwame's expectations were further shaped by the lobola negotiations, the bride price that his family had paid to Amina's family. This transaction, while customary, reinforced the notion that Amina was a valuable asset, a prize to be won. It solidified Kwame's sense of ownership and his belief that Amina was now obligated to fulfill her duties as his wife.

He did not perceive Amina's silence or her occasional moments of introspection as signs of discontent or rebellion. Instead, he interpreted them as shyness or a natural deference to his authority. He believed that with time and patience, Amina would come to appreciate the security and stability that their marriage offered, and that she would eventually embrace her role with genuine affection.

Kwame was confident that he could provide Amina with a comfortable life, free from hardship and uncertainty. He envisioned a future filled with prosperity, respect, and the continuation of their family's legacy. He believed that their marriage would be a testament to the strength of tradition and the enduring power of familial bonds.

Unbeknownst to Kwame, Amina harbored secret desires and yearnings that clashed with his traditional expectations. She longed for a love that was based on mutual respect, shared dreams, and genuine affection, not on duty or obligation. She questioned the power dynamics at play and wondered if she could ever truly be happy in a marriage that was not of her own choosing.

As the wedding day drew nearer, Kwame remained oblivious to Amina's internal turmoil, confident that their union would be a success. He prepared for his role as a husband and head of household, eager to embrace the responsibilities and privileges that came with his position. He was ready to build a life with Amina, a life that was rooted in tradition, respect, and the unwavering belief in the importance of family.

But fate, as it often does, had other plans in store for Kwame and Amina, plans that would challenge their beliefs, test their loyalties, and ultimately redefine the meaning of love, family, and tradition.

CHAPTER: 3
LOVE IN THE SHADOWS

The weight of expectation pressed down on Amina, the impending lobola negotiations looming large. Yet, amidst the suffocating atmosphere of tradition, a flicker of rebellion ignited within her soul. It was a dangerous flame, fueled by stolen glances and whispered promises, a flame that threatened to consume everything she held dear. Malik, with his unwavering gaze and gentle touch, was the forbidden fuel that kept it burning.

Their stolen moments were fragments of paradise carved out from the rigid structure of their lives. A clandestine meeting by the riverbank, where the water mirrored their longing. A hushed conversation beneath the ancient baobab tree, its roots as deep and intertwined as their feelings. Each encounter was a risk, a gamble with their futures, but the magnetic pull between them was too strong to resist.

The marketplace, usually a vibrant tapestry of sights and sounds, became a minefield of potential exposure. Amina would scan the crowd, her heart pounding in her chest, searching for Malik's familiar face. A fleeting touch, a brush of hands as they passed each other, was enough to send shivers down her spine and reaffirm their secret pact.

One evening, under the cloak of a star-studded sky, they met in the sacred grove, a place where the spirits of their ancestors were said to dwell. The air was thick with anticipation, the silence broken only by the chirping of crickets and the rustling of leaves. They spoke of their dreams, their hopes for a future where their love wouldn't be a crime.

"I can't imagine a life without you, Amina," Malik confessed, his voice raw with emotion. "But I won't let you sacrifice yourself for me. If it means defying your family, facing exile, I'll understand."

Amina's eyes welled up with tears. "And if I choose you, Malik? If I abandon my duty, my family's honor?" Her voice trembled with uncertainty.

"Then we'll face the consequences together," he vowed, his hand gently caressing her cheek. "We'll build a new life, a life where love is celebrated, not condemned."

Their whispered conversations were interlaced with fervent kisses, desperate embraces that spoke volumes of their yearning. In those stolen moments, they were free, unbound by the chains of tradition, their love a sanctuary from the storm brewing around them.

But the idyllic bubble they had created was fragile, threatened by the ever-present danger of discovery. Each stolen moment was a step closer to the precipice, a gamble with their hearts and their futures.

The weight of their secret grew heavier with each passing day, casting a shadow over Amina's every action. She found herself constantly on edge, her senses heightened, fearing the inevitable moment when their love would be exposed.

Despite the risks, they continued to meet, drawn together by an irresistible force. Their love was a beacon in the darkness, a symbol of hope in a world where tradition often stifled the human spirit. It was a love worth fighting for, a love worth risking everything for.

These clandestine encounters became the lifeblood of their souls, sustaining them amidst the suffocating expectations and looming uncertainties. They were moments of pure, unadulterated connection, where their hearts beat as one, defying the rigid boundaries of their predetermined lives. The passion between them intensified, fueled by the danger and the desperation, forging an unbreakable bond that transcended the constraints of their society.

In the quiet solitude of their secret rendezvous, they shared dreams of a future where their love could flourish without fear or judgment. They envisioned a life where they could build a home, raise a family, and celebrate their love openly, without the shadow of tradition looming over them. These dreams were the seeds of hope that they nurtured in the fertile ground of their hearts, providing them with the strength to face the challenges that lay ahead.

Yet, the idyllic nature of their stolen moments was constantly threatened by the harsh reality of their circumstances. The fear of discovery loomed large, casting a pall over their every encounter. They knew that their secret could not remain hidden forever, and the consequences of its exposure would be devastating. Still, they clung to each other, finding solace and strength in their shared love, determined to defy the odds and forge their own destiny.

As their love deepened, so did the stakes. The potential consequences of their actions became more severe, the risks more daunting. But their hearts were intertwined, their souls bound together by a force that transcended the boundaries of tradition and societal expectations. They were willing to face whatever challenges lay ahead, united in their love and their determination to create a future where their hearts could finally be free.

The weight of her secret pressed down on Amina, a suffocating blanket woven with stolen glances and whispered promises. She knew she couldn't carry it alone any longer. The joy she found in Malik's presence was undeniable, a vibrant flame that warmed her from the inside out, but the fear of discovery was a constant shadow, chilling her to the bone. She needed someone to confide in, someone who could understand the impossible situation she found herself in, caught between the love of her heart and the expectations of her family.

Her thoughts turned to Zuri, her younger cousin. Zuri was different, a spark of rebellious energy in a village steeped in tradition. Amina had always admired her spirit, her refusal to blindly accept the way things were. Zuri

Zuri reached out and took Amina's hand, her touch offering a silent reassurance. "I don't know, Amina. I truly don't. But you have to be careful. They're watching you, waiting for you to slip up. One wrong move, and everything could fall apart."

The weight of Zuri's warning settled heavily on Amina. She knew that every stolen moment with Malik, every secret rendezvous, was a gamble with potentially devastating consequences. The stakes were higher than just her own happiness; they involved the reputation and well-being of her entire family.

"I understand," Amina said, her voice barely audible. "I'll be careful. I promise." But even as she spoke the words, a flicker of defiance ignited within her. She couldn't deny her love for Malik, couldn't simply extinguish the flame that burned so brightly within her heart. She would be cautious, yes, but she wouldn't surrender. She would find a way to navigate the treacherous currents of tradition and societal expectations, to carve out a space for her love to flourish.

Zuri squeezed Amina's hand, her eyes filled with a mixture of concern and admiration. She knew that Amina was walking a dangerous path, one fraught with peril and uncertainty. But she also knew that Amina was strong, resourceful, and fiercely determined. If anyone could find a way to reconcile her love for Malik with her duty to her family, it was Amina.

"Just… please be careful, Amina," Zuri pleaded, her voice laced with genuine worry. "I don't want to see you get hurt. I don't want to see our family torn apart."

Amina nodded, her gaze fixed on the distant horizon. The challenges ahead were daunting, the risks immense. But she was no longer willing to simply accept the life that had been chosen for her. She would fight for her love, for her happiness, for her right to choose her own destiny. And she would do everything in her power to protect her family from the fallout of her decisions, even if it meant walking a tightrope between tradition and her own heart.

The conversation with Zuri served as a stark reminder of the precariousness of her situation. It was a sobering dose of reality that tempered the euphoria of her secret romance. Amina knew that she couldn't afford to be reckless or naive. She had to be strategic, discreet, and constantly aware of the watchful eyes that surrounded her.

As Amina lay in bed that night, the weight of Zuri's warning pressed down on her. The joy of her stolen moments with Malik was now tinged with a sense of anxiety and foreboding. She knew that their love was a fragile thing, easily shattered by the harsh realities of their world. But she also knew that it was worth fighting for, worth risking everything for. And with that conviction burning in her heart, she drifted off to sleep, dreaming of a future where love and tradition could coexist in harmony.

Amina knew the risks. Every stolen glance, every whispered word, every secret rendezvous carried the weight of potential devastation. To love Malik was to gamble with her entire future, to place her family's honor, her community standing, and her very identity on the altar of a forbidden desire. Yet, in his presence, the potential consequences seemed distant, overshadowed by the intoxicating allure of a connection that resonated deep within her soul.

The village, with its intricate web of traditions and expectations, left little room for individual desires that strayed from the prescribed path. Marriages were not merely unions of two hearts but strategic alliances, cementing family ties, consolidating wealth, and ensuring the continuation of ancestral legacies. To defy such a system was to invite not only personal ruin but also the wrath of an entire community.

Amina had witnessed firsthand the ostracization of those who dared to challenge the established order. Whispers followed them like shadows, doors closed in their faces, and their families bore the brunt of the community's disapproval. The fear of such a fate gnawed at her, a constant reminder of the precariousness of her situation.

Yet, the alternative – a life devoid of love, a marriage built on duty rather than affection – was equally terrifying. The thought of spending her days with Kwame, a man she respected but did not love, filled her with a sense of suffocating emptiness. It was a slow, silent death of the spirit, a sacrifice of her own happiness for the sake of tradition.

Malik, too, understood the gravity of their situation. He was an outsider, a self-made man who had earned his place in the village through hard work and determination. He lacked the lineage and connections that would make him an acceptable suitor for Amina, and he knew that their love was a direct challenge to the established social hierarchy.

He bore the weight of his own sacrifices. He risked the scorn of the community, the loss of his livelihood, and the potential for violence. Yet, he refused to relinquish his love for Amina, believing that their connection was worth fighting for, even if it meant defying the entire world.

Their secret meetings became a sanctuary, a space where they could shed the constraints of their predetermined roles and simply be themselves. They shared their dreams, their fears, and their hopes for a future where love reigned supreme, unburdened by the weight of tradition. In those moments, the risks seemed insignificant, the sacrifices bearable.

But the reality of their situation was never far from their minds. The whispers of the village, the watchful eyes of their families, and the ever-present threat of discovery cast a long shadow over their stolen moments of happiness. They knew that their love was a fragile flame, easily extinguished by the winds of societal disapproval.

Amina often found herself torn between her love for Malik and her duty to her family. She yearned to break free from the constraints of tradition, to forge her own path in life, but she also feared the consequences of her actions. The thought of causing her family pain, of bringing shame upon their name, weighed heavily on her heart.

Malik, sensing her internal conflict, offered her unwavering support. He never pressured her to choose him over her family, understanding the depth of her loyalty and the complexity of her situation. He simply promised to stand by her, no matter what the future held, and to love her with all his heart.

Their love became a rebellion, a quiet act of defiance against a system that sought to control their destinies. They found strength in each other's arms, vowing to protect their love at all costs, even if it meant sacrificing everything they had ever known. They were two souls intertwined, bound together by a love that defied tradition and challenged the very foundations of their society.

The sacrifices were already mounting. Stolen moments replaced family gatherings, whispered conversations replaced open laughter, and the constant fear of discovery cast a pall over their lives. Yet, in their hearts, they knew that their love was worth the price, a beacon of hope in a world governed by tradition and expectation. The path ahead was fraught with danger, but they were determined to walk it together, hand in hand, hearts ablaze with a love that refused to be denied.

Beyond the stolen glances and hushed whispers, Amina and Malik found solace in shared dreams. Their clandestine meetings, often under the cloak of twilight near the whispering river, weren't merely fueled by forbidden desire. They were a communion of souls, a recognition of kindred spirits yearning for a world beyond the rigid confines of their village.

Malik, with his calloused hands and eyes that held the vastness of the open sky, spoke of a future where hard work and determination, not lineage, defined a man. He envisioned a life where he could provide for Amina, not with inherited wealth, but with the fruits of his own labor. He dreamt of a small farm, where they could cultivate the land and raise a family free from the suffocating expectations of their elders.

Amina, in turn, shared her aspirations, her voice barely a whisper above the rustling leaves. She yearned to use her education, her knowledge gleaned from the worn pages of her beloved books, to uplift the women in their community. She dreamt of a school where girls could learn to read and write, where they could discover their own potential and break free from the cycle of arranged marriages and subservient roles.

Their dreams, though seemingly simple, were revolutionary in their context. They challenged the very foundation upon which their society was built – a society where tradition reigned supreme and individual aspirations were often sacrificed at the altar of family honor. It was this shared vision, this mutual desire for a better future, that solidified their bond and transformed their forbidden attraction into something far deeper and more meaningful.

During one of their secret rendezvous, as the moon cast long shadows across the riverbank, Malik presented Amina with a small, intricately carved wooden bird. It was a symbol, he explained, of their shared desire for freedom, for the ability to soar above the limitations imposed upon them. Amina clutched the bird tightly, her heart swelling with a mixture of fear and hope.

"This is beautiful, Malik," she whispered, her voice thick with emotion. "But what if we can't fly? What if our wings are clipped before we even have a chance to take flight?"

Malik gently cupped her face in his hands, his eyes filled with unwavering resolve. "Then we will build stronger wings," he declared. "We will find a way, Amina. I promise you, we will find a way to make our dreams a reality."

Their shared faith also played a crucial role in strengthening their bond. They both found solace and guidance in their Christian beliefs, often discussing the scriptures and seeking divine wisdom in the face of their daunting challenges. They believed that God had brought them together for a reason, that their love was not a mere coincidence but a divine blessing.

However, their faith also presented a complex dilemma. While they found comfort in the teachings of love and compassion, they also grappled with the traditional interpretations that often reinforced the patriarchal structures of their society. They questioned whether blind obedience to tradition was truly in line with God's will, or whether they were called to challenge the status quo and forge their own path.

It was during these intimate conversations, under the watchful eyes of the stars, that Amina and Malik discovered the true depth of their connection. They were not merely lovers; they were confidantes, partners in crime, and fellow pilgrims on a journey towards a more just and equitable world. Their shared values and dreams for the future became the bedrock upon which their forbidden love was built, a foundation strong enough to withstand the storms that lay ahead.

Their love was a beacon of hope, a testament to the power of individual agency in the face of overwhelming societal pressure. It was a dangerous flame, flickering in the shadows, but it was also a source of warmth and light, illuminating the path towards a future where love, not tradition, would guide their destinies.

As their bond deepened, Amina found herself increasingly torn between her love for Malik and her duty to her family. The weight of expectation pressed heavily upon her shoulders, threatening to crush her spirit. She knew that defying her family's wishes would have dire consequences, but she also knew that she could not deny the truth in her heart. She loved Malik, and she was willing to risk everything for a chance at a life filled with love and happiness.

Malik, too, felt the immense pressure of their situation. He knew that he was asking Amina to sacrifice everything for him, to abandon her family and her community. He wrestled with guilt and self-doubt, questioning whether he was worthy of such a profound sacrifice. But he also knew that he could not live without her, that she was the missing piece of his soul, the light that guided him through the darkness.

Their love was a dangerous rebellion, a challenge to the established order, but it was also a testament to the enduring power of the human spirit. It was a story of courage, of sacrifice, and of unwavering faith in the face of adversity. And as they stood together, hand in hand, under the watchful eyes of the African sky, they knew that their journey was far from over, that the true test of their love was yet to come.

CHAPTER: 4

A DEAL SEALED IN BLOOD

The day arrived with a heavy, almost suffocating atmosphere. It wasn't the weather, which was bright and clear, typical of the season, but the air itself seemed thick with unspoken expectations and the weight of generations. Today, the lobola negotiations would begin. Amina felt a knot tightening in her stomach, a cold dread that settled deep in her bones. This wasn't a celebration; it was a transaction, a deal being struck over her future.

The men gathered in the courtyard of her family's compound, their voices a low rumble that carried through the open windows. Mansa, her grandfather and the family patriarch, sat at the head of the table, his posture ramrod straight, his face an impassive mask. He was a man of few words, but his presence commanded respect, even fear. He embodied tradition, a living embodiment of the customs that had shaped their family for centuries.

Across from him sat the delegation from Kwame's family, equally stern and unyielding. They were powerful men, landowners and respected elders in the community. Amina knew that these negotiations were not just about her;

they were about solidifying alliances, securing the family's future, and maintaining their position in the village hierarchy.

The air crackled with tension as the negotiations began. The men spoke in measured tones, their words carefully chosen, each phrase laden with meaning. They discussed the value of the bride, not in terms of her beauty or intelligence, but in terms of her worth to the family. Her ability to bear children, her skills in the home, her contribution to the family's standing in the community – all were weighed and measured, quantified into a price.

Amina felt a wave of nausea wash over her. She was not a person, not a woman with dreams and desires, but a commodity to be traded, a pawn in a game played by men. Her heart ached with a longing for Malik, for a love that was not based on obligation or tradition, but on mutual respect and affection. But Malik was not here, and his absence was a painful reminder of the chasm that separated them.

Mansa, with his deep, resonant voice, led the negotiations for her family. He was a formidable opponent, a shrewd negotiator who knew how to drive a hard bargain. He spoke of Amina's virtues, exaggerating her skills and accomplishments, painting a picture of the perfect wife, the ideal daughter-in-law. Amina felt a strange sense of detachment, as if she were watching a play unfold, a drama in which she was both the protagonist and a mere spectator.

The lobola, the bride price, was not simply a monetary exchange; it was a symbolic gesture, a recognition of the value of the woman and the loss her family would suffer upon her departure. It was a way of compensating them for the years they had invested in raising her, for the contribution she would have made to their household. But to Amina, it felt like a transaction, a cold, calculated assessment of her worth.

As the negotiations dragged on, Amina's despair deepened. She felt trapped, her fate seemingly sealed by the decisions of these men. She longed to escape, to run away from the suffocating weight of tradition, but she knew that such an act would bring shame and dishonor upon her family. She was caught in a web of obligation, bound by the chains of duty.

The price Mansa demanded was high, a testament to his pride and his determination to secure the best possible future for his family. He asked for cattle, goats, land, and precious metals – a king's ransom for his granddaughter. Amina wondered if Kwame was worth such a price, if any man was worth sacrificing her happiness for.

The sun began to set, casting long shadows across the courtyard. The negotiations continued, the men haggling and bargaining, their voices growing hoarse with fatigue. Amina felt a sense of numbness creeping over her, a detachment from the proceedings. She had lost all hope of escape, all belief in a different future. Her fate was sealed, her life no longer her own.

As the stars began to appear in the night sky, the negotiations finally came to a close. A price had been agreed upon, a deal struck. Amina was now officially betrothed to Kwame, her future determined by the decisions of men who saw her as nothing more than a commodity. She felt a profound sense of loss, a deep ache in her heart. Her dreams, her hopes, her desires – all had been sacrificed on the altar of tradition.

She retreated to her room, the weight of her impending marriage crushing her spirit. The walls seemed to close in on her, suffocating her with their silence. She sank to her knees, tears streaming down her face. Her heart cried out for Malik, for the love that could never be. But even as she wept, a flicker of defiance ignited within her. She would not surrender completely. She would find a way to survive, to preserve her spirit, even in the face of this crushing defeat.

The air in the room crackled with unspoken tension. Amina sat silently, her hands clasped tightly in her lap, as the lobola negotiations unfolded around her. The rhythmic cadence of Mansa's voice, usually a comforting sound, now echoed like a relentless drumbeat, each word a hammer blow against her heart. She watched as her grandfather, the patriarch of their family, bartered for her future, haggling over cows, land, and promises of prosperity. It felt as though she were an object, a prized possession to be exchanged, rather than a woman with dreams and desires of her own.

Kwame's family, represented by his uncles and elder brothers, countered Mansa's demands with measured responses, their faces stoic and unreadable. Amina tried to decipher their expressions, searching for any sign of empathy or understanding, but found only the cold, hard glint of tradition. She was a pawn in their game, a means to an end, a symbol of the alliance they sought to forge between their families. The weight of their expectations pressed down on her, suffocating her spirit and stealing her breath.

Each offer and counter-offer felt like a brand seared into her soul, marking her as property to be owned and controlled. The vibrant colors of her traditional attire, usually a source of pride, now seemed like a costume, a disguise that concealed her true self. She longed to tear it off, to shed the weight of tradition and reveal the woman beneath, the woman who yearned for love, for freedom, for a life of her own choosing.

Amina glanced at her mother, hoping to find solace in her eyes, but Jamila's gaze was fixed on Mansa, her expression a mixture of pride and resignation. Amina knew her mother understood her plight, but she also knew that Jamila was bound by the same traditions, the same expectations that held Amina captive. There was no escape, no refuge, no one to fight for her cause.

The negotiations continued, the voices rising and falling in a hypnotic rhythm that lulled Amina into a state of despair. She felt herself drifting away, her spirit separating from her body, watching the scene unfold as if it were a play, a tragic drama in which she was the unwilling protagonist. She was a commodity, a currency to be exchanged, her worth measured in livestock and land.

Tears welled up in her eyes, blurring her vision, but she refused to let them fall. She would not give them the satisfaction of seeing her break, of witnessing her surrender. She would remain strong, even in the face of this injustice, even as her future was being bartered away before her very eyes.

The realization washed over her, cold and stark: she was being sold. Not in the literal sense, perhaps, but in every way that mattered. Her dreams, her hopes, her very essence were being traded for the sake of family honor and social standing. The vibrant tapestry of her life was being reduced to a transaction, a business deal devoid of love, compassion, or understanding.

Amina's heart ached with a profound sense of loss. She mourned the life she had envisioned for herself, the life filled with love and laughter, with shared dreams and mutual respect. That life was now slipping away, replaced by a future of obligation and duty, a future in which she would be nothing more than a wife, a mother, a servant to her husband and his family.

The weight of her predicament settled upon her like a shroud, suffocating her spirit and extinguishing the flame of hope that had flickered within her. She felt like a bird trapped in a cage, its wings clipped, its song silenced. She was a prisoner of tradition, bound by chains of expectation and duty.

In that moment, Amina understood the true cost of tradition, the sacrifices it demanded, the dreams it crushed. She knew that she could not simply accept her fate, that she had to fight for her own happiness, even if it meant defying her family and challenging the very foundations of her society. The seed of rebellion had been planted, and she knew that it would soon blossom into a force that could not be contained.

The faces around the room swam before her eyes, a blur of expectation and tradition. Each word spoken, each nod of agreement, felt like another nail hammered into the coffin of her dreams. She was a prize to be won, a possession to be bartered, her own desires and aspirations rendered invisible in the face of ancient customs.

Amina closed her eyes, focusing on the image of Malik, his face a beacon of hope in the encroaching darkness. His love was the only thing that kept her tethered to reality, the only thing that reminded her of her own worth. She clung to that image, drawing strength from his unwavering belief in her, his unwavering belief in their love.

The negotiations droned on, oblivious to the turmoil raging within her. She was a silent observer, a ghost in her own life, watching as her future was decided by others. The injustice of it all burned within her, a slow, simmering rage that threatened to erupt at any moment.

Amina knew that she could not remain silent any longer. She had to speak, to assert her own will, to reclaim her own destiny. The time for obedience was over. The time for rebellion had come.

She would find a way out. She had to. Her spirit, though wounded, was not broken. The fire of her faith, though dimmed, still flickered. And the love in her heart, though threatened, still burned bright. She would not surrender.

She would not be silenced. She would fight for her own happiness, even if it meant standing alone against the world.

The air in the kraal hung heavy with the unspoken agreement, the silent bartering of her future. Each nod, each murmured price, felt like another brick in the wall sealing her fate. Amina watched, detached, as Mansa, her grandfather, negotiated with Kwame's uncles. The lobola, the bride price, was more than just a transaction; it was a testament to her worth, a symbol of the bond between two families. But to Amina, it felt like she was a prized cow being traded for prestige and security.

The weight of expectation pressed down on her, suffocating her spirit. She understood the tradition, the importance of securing her family's future, but at what cost? Was her happiness worth so little? Was her voice so insignificant that it could be bartered away without a second thought? The vibrant colors of her traditional attire seemed to mock her, a beautiful cage trapping her within its intricate design.

The negotiations dragged on, each point meticulously debated, each concession carefully considered. Amina felt like a ghost in her own life, watching from a distance as her destiny was decided by others. The faces around her were etched with determination, their eyes focused on securing the best possible deal. No one seemed to notice the turmoil raging within her, the silent screams for freedom that echoed in her heart.

As the sun began to dip below the horizon, casting long shadows across the kraal, Amina slipped away unnoticed. She sought refuge in the small, secluded prayer room behind her grandmother's hut. The room was simple, adorned only with a worn wooden cross and a small, hand-stitched tapestry depicting the Last Supper. It was here, in this quiet sanctuary, that Amina found solace and strength.

She knelt before the cross, her heart heavy with despair. Tears streamed down her face as she poured out her anguish to God. She pleaded for guidance, for a sign, for a way out of this impossible situation. "Oh, Lord," she whispered, her voice choked with emotion, "show me the path. Give me the strength to do what is right, even if it means defying tradition, even if it means breaking my family's heart."

The weight of the impending marriage felt like a physical burden, crushing her beneath its immense pressure. She closed her eyes, picturing Malik's face, his warm smile, the way his eyes sparkled when he spoke of their dreams. Could she truly abandon him, sacrifice their love for the sake of duty? The thought was unbearable, a dagger twisting in her heart.

She remembered Jabulani's words, her uncle's quiet warning: "A marriage without love is a house without a foundation." His words resonated with her, confirming the doubts that had been gnawing at her soul. She knew that marrying Kwame would be a betrayal of her own heart, a slow, agonizing death of her spirit.

But defying her family, breaking the sacred traditions of her ancestors, was a daunting prospect. The shame, the ostracism, the pain she would inflict on those she loved – it was almost too much to bear. She wrestled with her conscience, torn between her duty to her family and her yearning for personal freedom.

As she knelt in prayer, a sense of calm washed over her, a quiet assurance that she was not alone. She felt God's presence surrounding her, comforting her, guiding her. A verse from the Bible came to mind, a passage her grandmother often recited: "Trust in the Lord with all your heart, and lean not on your own understanding; in all your ways submit to him, and he will make your paths straight." (Proverbs 3:5-6)

Amina clung to those words, finding strength in their promise. She knew that the path ahead would be difficult, fraught with challenges and heartache. But she also knew that she could not betray her own heart, that she could not live a life devoid of love and happiness. She would trust in God's guidance, and she would find a way to honor her family while also pursuing her own destiny.

The weight on her chest didn't disappear, but it felt lighter, more bearable. She would face the coming days with courage, with faith, and with the unwavering belief that God would lead her to the right decision. She would not be a passive victim, a commodity to be traded. She would fight for her own happiness, for her own voice, for her own future.

Emerging from the prayer room, Amina carried a newfound resolve within her. The negotiations were still underway, the voices still droning on, but she no longer felt like a detached observer. She was a participant in her own life, a warrior ready to fight for her heart's desire. The battle was far from over, but she was no longer afraid. She had faith, and she had love, and that was enough to face whatever lay ahead.

The practice of lobola, the bride price, was as old as the hills that cradled their village. It was more than just a transaction; it was a deeply woven tapestry of respect, obligation, and the symbolic union of two families. Amina knew this, had grown up hearing tales of her own mother's lobola, the cows, goats, and blankets exchanged to signify her worth and the bond created between her family and her father's.

But today, as she sat listening to the hushed tones of the men negotiating her own price, a chilling realization washed over her. She wasn't a daughter being honored; she was a commodity being traded. Every cow, every goat, every meticulously woven blanket felt like a piece of her soul being bartered away. The weight of tradition, once a comforting blanket, now felt like a suffocating shroud.

Lobola, in its purest form, was meant to be a gesture of goodwill, a way for the groom's family to show their appreciation for the bride and to compensate her family for the loss of her labor and companionship. It was a symbol of commitment, a promise that the groom would take care of his wife and provide for her needs. But somewhere along the way, Amina thought, the true meaning had been lost, twisted into a measure of a woman's worth in material terms.

She glanced at her mother, seated a respectful distance away, her face etched with a mixture of pride and resignation. Did her mother feel this way too, all those years ago? Had she felt like a prized possession, a valuable asset being transferred from one family to another? Amina couldn't bring herself to ask. The unspoken rules of their society forbade such questions, such displays of discontent.

The women of the village, Amina knew, held a complex relationship with lobola. On one hand, it provided a sense of security, a validation of their importance within the community. A high lobola could elevate a family's status, bringing them respect and influence. It also served as a form of social security; in the event of divorce or widowhood, the lobola could provide a woman with the means to support herself and her children.

But on the other hand, lobola reinforced the patriarchal structure of their society, perpetuating the idea that women were property to be owned and controlled. It limited their choices, their autonomy, and their ability to determine their own destinies. A woman's value was often tied to her ability to bear children, particularly sons, further diminishing her worth as an individual.

Amina thought of Nandi, a woman in the village who had been ostracized after her husband died. Her lobola had been meager, and her husband's family had refused to provide for her, claiming she was no longer their responsibility. Nandi had been left destitute, forced to beg for scraps and endure the scorn of the community. Amina shuddered at the thought of suffering a similar fate.

The negotiations continued, the men haggling over the number of cattle and the quality of the blankets. Amina felt her spirit shrinking, her voice fading into the background noise of tradition. She longed to speak out, to challenge the system, to declare her own worth independent of material possessions. But fear held her back, the fear of shame, of ostracism, of betraying her family.

Jabulani, her uncle, caught her eye and offered a small, almost imperceptible nod of encouragement. He understood her struggle, her inner turmoil. He had always been a champion of women's rights, a quiet rebel who questioned the status quo. But even he was bound by the constraints of tradition, unable to openly defy the elders.

Amina closed her eyes, seeking solace in her faith. She prayed for guidance, for strength, for a way out of this suffocating predicament. Was it possible to honor her family and her traditions while still pursuing her own happiness? Was there a middle ground, a path that would allow her to reconcile her duty with her desires?

The answer, she knew, wouldn't come easily. It would require courage, resilience, and a willingness to challenge the very foundations of her society.

But as she sat there, listening to the rhythmic chanting of the negotiators, a spark of defiance ignited within her. She was more than just a bride price; she was a woman with dreams, with aspirations, with a heart that yearned for love. And she wouldn't let tradition extinguish her flame.

The sun beat down on the courtyard, casting long shadows that danced like restless spirits. Amina knew that the days ahead would be filled with uncertainty and conflict. But she also knew that she wasn't alone. She had her faith, her family, and the unwavering support of Malik, the man who saw her for who she truly was, not just for what she was worth.

Mansa, the family patriarch, was a man carved from the very bedrock of tradition. His face, etched with the stories of generations past, held a sternness that brooked no argument when it came to upholding the customs of their ancestors. He was the embodiment of the village's collective memory, the living link to a time when life was simpler, when roles were clearly defined, and when the family's honor was paramount above all else.

The lobola negotiations were not merely a transaction to Mansa; they were a sacred ritual, a reaffirmation of the bond between two families, a guarantee of Amina's well-being in her new home. It was a practice steeped in history, a testament to the value placed on women within their community. To him, it was an insult to suggest that it was a mere exchange of money for a bride. It was far more profound than that.

He saw Amina's marriage to Kwame as more than just a union of two individuals; it was a strategic alliance, a strengthening of their family's position within the village. Kwame's family was influential, their wealth and power undeniable. A union between them would ensure the prosperity and security of Mansa's lineage for generations to come. This was not about personal happiness; it was about the greater good of the family.

Mansa had always envisioned a bright future for Amina, one where she would be respected, protected, and provided for. He believed that Kwame, with his strong character and his deep roots in the community, was the perfect man to offer her such a life. He couldn't fathom why Amina couldn't see the wisdom in his decision, why she couldn't understand the sacrifices he was making for her sake.

He remembered his own arranged marriage, a union that had initially been met with apprehension but had blossomed into a deep and abiding love. He believed that love could be cultivated, that it was a choice, a commitment, not merely a fleeting emotion. He had faith that Amina would come to love Kwame, just as he had come to love his own wife.

As the negotiations progressed, Mansa's demands grew more stringent. He wanted to ensure that Amina would be treated with the utmost respect, that her needs would be met, and that her future would be secure. He saw it as his duty to extract the highest possible lobola, not out of greed, but out of a deep-seated desire to protect his granddaughter.

He was aware of the whispers circulating within the village, the rumors of Amina's affections for Malik, the outsider. He dismissed them as mere infatuations, fleeting fancies that would fade with time. He refused to believe that Amina would jeopardize her family's honor for the sake of a forbidden love.

Mansa was a man of unwavering conviction, a man who believed in the sanctity of tradition, a man who would do anything to protect his family's future. He was a product of his time, a reflection of the values and beliefs that had shaped his life. He could not comprehend Amina's desire for personal freedom, her yearning for a love that defied the boundaries of tradition.

He saw her rebellion as a betrayal, a rejection of everything he held dear. He couldn't understand why she couldn't see the wisdom in his decisions, why she couldn't appreciate the sacrifices he was making for her sake. He was determined to guide her back onto the right path, to steer her away from the dangerous allure of forbidden love.

Mansa's adherence to tradition was not merely a matter of personal preference; it was a deeply ingrained belief that the customs of their ancestors were the foundation of their society, the glue that held their community together. To abandon those traditions would be to invite chaos, to unravel the fabric of their existence. He was the guardian of those traditions, the protector of their way of life, and he would not allow Amina to jeopardize everything he held dear.

CHAPTER: 5

A FORBIDDEN GOODBYE

Malik stared out at the familiar landscape, the rolling hills that cradled their village now seeming like prison walls. The weight of their forbidden love pressed down on him, suffocating any hope of a future within these confines. Every stolen glance, every whispered promise, every secret rendezvous now felt like a cruel taunt, a reminder of what they could never openly have.

He had wrestled with the agonizing truth for weeks, the realization dawning upon him like a slow, creeping sunrise. Amina was bound by duty, by tradition, by the invisible chains of family honor. He, on the other hand, was an outsider, a man with no lineage, no wealth, no standing in their rigid society. Their love was a rebellion, a dangerous spark in a world that demanded conformity.

The lobola negotiations had been the final nail in the coffin. The exorbitant price Mansa demanded for Amina's hand was a clear message: she was a commodity, a valuable asset to be bartered and traded. Malik knew, with a sickening certainty, that he could never afford her, not in the eyes of her family. He was a self-made man, but his worth was measured in different terms, terms that held no value in this world.

He couldn't bear to watch Amina wither away, trapped in a loveless marriage, her spirit slowly extinguished by the weight of expectation. He loved her too much to subject her to that fate. And so, with a heart heavier than any stone, he made a decision. He would leave.

He would leave the village, the only home he had ever known, and create a new life for himself, a life where he could offer Amina a genuine chance at happiness. It was a desperate gamble, a leap of faith into the unknown. But he clung to the hope that she would follow him, that her love for him was strong enough to break the chains that bound her.

He imagined her face, the mixture of shock and sorrow that would undoubtedly cloud her beautiful eyes when he told her his plan. He knew it would be a painful conversation, a tearful goodbye. But he also knew that it was the only way, the only path that offered even a glimmer of hope for their future.

He would leave a message for her, a carefully worded plea, etched onto a piece of bark from the ancient tree where they had shared their first kiss. He would tell her that he was going to the city, to find work, to build a life for them. He would tell her that he would wait for her, patiently, endlessly, until the day she was ready to join him.

He knew the risks were immense. If she chose to follow him, she would be ostracized, disowned, branded as a disgrace to her family. But he also knew that Amina possessed a strength, a quiet resilience that belied her gentle nature. He had seen it in her eyes, in the way she challenged her family's expectations, in the way she dared to love him, despite the consequences.

He trusted her, he believed in her, and he prayed that she would find the courage to choose love over duty, to choose freedom over tradition. He knew it was a selfish request, a heavy burden to place upon her shoulders. But he also knew that their love was worth fighting for, worth sacrificing for, worth risking everything for.

As the sun began to set, casting long shadows across the valley, Malik prepared to leave. He packed a small bag with the few possessions he owned, his heart aching with every step. He paused at the edge of the village, gazing back at the familiar rooftops, the smoke curling from the chimneys, the sounds of laughter and music drifting on the evening breeze. He was leaving a part of himself behind, a part that he would never forget.

He whispered a silent prayer, a plea for guidance, for strength, for Amina's safety. And then, with a deep breath, he turned his back on the village and walked towards the unknown, his heart filled with both hope and trepidation. The path ahead was uncertain, but one thing was clear: he was doing it for love, for Amina, for the chance to build a future where their love could finally blossom, free from the constraints of tradition and expectation.

He knew that his decision would set in motion a chain of events that would forever alter the course of their lives. But he also knew that sometimes, the greatest acts of love required the greatest sacrifices. And he was willing to sacrifice everything, if it meant that Amina could finally be free.

Malik's words hung in the air, a promise and a plea woven together. He would leave, not to abandon her, but to create a space where their love might exist without the suffocating weight of tradition. He envisioned a life where Amina could be free, where her spirit wouldn't be crushed under the expectations of a society that valued obedience over happiness. But the thought of leaving her family, her village, the only world she had ever known, was a heavy burden for Amina to bear.

The weight of her decision pressed down on her, a physical ache in her chest. Every fiber of her being yearned to run, to escape the gilded cage that tradition had built around her. To be with Malik, to breathe the air of freedom, to choose her own destiny – the allure was undeniable. Yet, the faces of her family swam before her eyes – her grandmother Jamila, with her gentle wisdom; her younger siblings, who looked up to her; even her stern grandfather, Mansa, whose approval she had always craved. Could she truly abandon them?

The concept of exile was a chilling one. It wasn't merely about leaving a place; it was about severing ties, about becoming an outsider, a pariah. The village was more than just a collection of houses; it was a web of relationships, of shared history, of mutual support. To be exiled meant to be cut off from that web, to be adrift in a world where she knew no one, where she had no roots. The thought of facing such isolation was terrifying.

Amina sought solace in the quiet corners of her home, in the familiar rhythm of daily life that suddenly felt fragile and fleeting. She helped her mother prepare meals, her hands moving mechanically as her mind wrestled with the impossible choice. She listened to the laughter of her younger siblings, their carefree joy a stark contrast to the turmoil within her. Each interaction, each familiar sight and sound, tugged at her heart, making the prospect of leaving all the more agonizing.

She remembered Jabulani's words, spoken with a knowing sadness: "A marriage without love is a house without a foundation." He had seen her unhappiness, recognized the spark of rebellion in her eyes. But even he, with his progressive views, couldn't fully grasp the depth of her dilemma. He hadn't been raised with the same ingrained sense of duty, the same fear of dishonoring his family. His path had been different, less constrained by the rigid expectations of their community.

Amina visited the river, its gentle flow a constant presence in her life. She sat on its banks, watching the water ripple and dance in the sunlight, seeking guidance in its timeless wisdom. The river had witnessed generations of her family, their joys and sorrows, their triumphs and failures. It had been a source of sustenance, a place of reflection, a silent witness to the unfolding drama of their lives. Could she turn her back on that legacy?

She thought of Malik, his unwavering gaze, his gentle touch, the way he made her feel seen and understood. He wasn't just offering her love; he was offering her a chance to be herself, to break free from the mold that society had cast for her. He believed in her, in her strength, in her ability to forge her own path. And that belief, that unwavering faith in her potential, was a powerful force, pulling her towards him with irresistible force.

But the faces of her family haunted her dreams. She saw her mother's tear-streaked face, her father's disappointed gaze, her grandmother's pleading eyes. She heard their voices, whispering words of love and obligation, of tradition and duty. The weight of their expectations was a heavy chain, binding her to a life she didn't want, a future that felt like a prison.

Amina knew that whatever decision she made, it would come at a cost. There was no easy way out, no path that wouldn't lead to pain and sacrifice. To choose Malik meant to risk losing her family, her community, her sense of belonging. To choose her family meant to sacrifice her own happiness, to live a life of quiet desperation, to forever wonder what might have been.

The days that followed were a blur of conflicting emotions, of sleepless nights and tearful prayers. Amina was caught in a tempest, tossed and turned by the forces of love and duty, of tradition and desire. She felt like a ship lost at sea, with no compass to guide her, no lighthouse to lead her home. The decision she faced was not just about her own happiness; it was about the fate of her family, the future of her community, the very fabric of her world.

Malik's words echoed in Amina's mind, a siren's call promising a life painted with the vibrant hues of freedom and love. Yet, the familiar comfort of her village, the deep-rooted connections to her family, tugged at her heartstrings with equal force. The decision before her was a chasm, a gaping divide between the life she knew and the life she dared to dream.

The faces of her family swam before her eyes – Mansa, her grandfather, his stern gaze softened only by the faintest hint of affection; Jamila, her grandmother, her eyes crinkled with wisdom and love; her parents, their lives dedicated to upholding the traditions of their ancestors. Could she truly turn her back on them, sever the ties that bound her to their legacy?

The village itself, nestled in the heart of the valley, was more than just a place; it was an extension of her very being. Every stone, every tree, every familiar face held a memory, a piece of her history. To leave would be to tear a part of herself away, to become a stranger in a world that had always felt like home.

But then, Malik's face would appear, his eyes filled with a love that transcended tradition and societal expectations. He offered her a different kind of home, one built on mutual respect, shared dreams, and the freedom to be her true self. He saw beyond the constraints of her predetermined path, recognizing the fire that burned within her, the yearning for a life that was authentically her own.

The weight of her community's expectations pressed down on her, a heavy cloak threatening to suffocate her spirit. She knew the whispers that would follow her departure, the judgment that would be passed down through generations. To defy tradition was to invite shame, to become an outcast, a pariah in the eyes of her people.

Yet, the thought of marrying Kwame, a man chosen for her, not by her, filled her with a sense of dread. It was a life sentence, a gilded cage where her spirit would wither and die. Could she truly sacrifice her own happiness for the sake of family honor, for the sake of upholding a tradition that felt increasingly archaic and oppressive?

Sleep offered no respite, her dreams a chaotic jumble of faces and places, of whispered promises and tearful goodbyes. She tossed and turned, her mind racing, her heart aching with the impossible choice before her. Was love truly worth abandoning everything she had ever known?

She sought solace in the quiet solitude of the sacred grove, the ancient trees whispering secrets of resilience and strength. She prayed for guidance, for a sign, for some semblance of clarity in the midst of her turmoil. But the only answer she received was the echo of her own conflicted heart.

Zuri, her confidante, offered a sympathetic ear, but even her unwavering support couldn't ease Amina's burden. Zuri, caught in her own struggles with societal expectations, understood the allure of freedom, but also the fear of defying tradition. Her own path was fraught with challenges, and Amina couldn't bear the thought of influencing her cousin towards a similar fate.

Amina imagined the faces of the women who came before her, her grandmothers and great-grandmothers, their lives shaped by duty and sacrifice. Had they ever questioned their predetermined paths? Had they ever dared to dream of a different kind of life? Or had they simply accepted their fate with quiet resignation?

The thought of disappointing them, of breaking the chain of tradition, filled her with guilt. But then, she remembered Jabulani's words, his gentle reminder that a marriage without love was a house without a foundation. Could she truly build a life on a foundation of obligation and duty, without the mortar of love to hold it together?

The days that followed were a blur of internal debate, of whispered conversations with Malik, of tearful moments with her family. Each interaction only served to deepen her confusion, to amplify the impossible weight of her decision. She felt like a ship caught in a storm, tossed and turned by conflicting currents, with no clear direction in sight.

As Malik prepared to leave, a sense of urgency washed over Amina. Time was running out, and she knew that she couldn't remain suspended in this state of indecision forever. She had to choose, to embrace her destiny, whatever the consequences may be.

The village, the family, the traditions – they were all a part of her, woven into the very fabric of her being. But so was her love for Malik, a love that burned with a fierce intensity, a love that threatened to consume her if she denied it. The question was, could she reconcile these two opposing forces, or would she be forced to choose between them, forever sacrificing a part of herself in the process?

In the end, Amina knew that the decision was hers and hers alone. No one could make it for her, no one could bear the weight of its consequences. She had to listen to her heart, to trust her instincts, and to have faith that whatever path she chose, it would lead her to where she was meant to be. The only thing she was sure of was that the decision would change her life forever.

The weight of Malik's words settled upon Amina like a shroud. Leave? Abandon everything she had ever known? The thought was a tempest within her, a maelstrom of conflicting emotions threatening to tear her apart. Her village, her family, her faith – all were anchors tethering her to a life she had always accepted, a life that was now being challenged by the intoxicating promise of love.

She wandered to the riverbank, the familiar rush of water a constant, soothing presence. This was where she had played as a child, where she had shared secrets with Zuri, where she had come to find solace in times of trouble. Every stone, every tree, held a memory, a piece of her heart. Could she truly leave it all behind?

The faces of her family swam before her eyes. Mansa, her grandfather, his stern gaze softened only by the love he held for his grandchildren. Jamila, her grandmother, her gentle hands always ready to offer comfort and guidance. Her parents, their lives dedicated to upholding the traditions of their ancestors. How could she inflict such pain upon them? How could she betray their trust, their expectations?

And yet, the thought of a life without Malik was a desolate wasteland. His laughter, his touch, his unwavering belief in her – these were the things that made her soul sing. He saw her, truly saw her, beyond the expectations and obligations that had defined her existence. He offered her a chance to be herself, to choose her own destiny.

Tears streamed down her face, blurring the reflection of the setting sun on the water. Each drop was a testament to the agonizing choice that lay before her. To stay meant a life of quiet desperation, a slow erosion of her spirit. To leave meant severing ties that had bound her for generations, a leap into the unknown with no guarantee of happiness.

She thought of Jabulani, her uncle, his words echoing in her mind: "A marriage without love is a house without a foundation." He had always encouraged her to think for herself, to question the status quo. But even he could not fully comprehend the depth of her dilemma, the cultural and familial forces that were pulling her in opposite directions.

The village, with its familiar rhythms and comforting certainties, was also a cage. The expectations, the judgments, the unspoken rules – they had shaped her into someone she no longer recognized. Malik offered her a key, a chance to unlock the door and step into a world of her own making.

But freedom came at a price. Exile. Shame. Disgrace. These were the words that haunted her, whispered by the wind through the trees. Could she bear the weight of such consequences? Could she live with the knowledge that she had shattered her family's honor?

She closed her eyes, seeking guidance from her faith. But even God seemed silent, leaving her to navigate this treacherous path alone. Was it selfish to choose her own happiness? Was it a sin to defy the traditions that had sustained her community for centuries?

The river flowed on, indifferent to her turmoil. The sun dipped below the horizon, casting long shadows that danced like demons in her mind. The weight of her decision pressed down on her, threatening to suffocate her. She was caught between two worlds, two loves, two destinies. And the choice, ultimately, was hers alone.

As darkness enveloped the valley, Amina knew she couldn't stay by the river forever. She had to face her family, face Malik, and face the truth within her own heart. The path ahead was fraught with peril, but she could no longer deny the yearning for something more, something real, something that resonated with the deepest part of her soul.

The emotional turmoil was a physical ache, a constant knot in her stomach. She imagined the whispers, the stares, the condemnation that would follow her if she chose to leave. She pictured her mother's tear-streaked face, her father's disappointed silence. The guilt was a heavy burden, almost too much to bear.

Yet, beneath the guilt and the fear, a flicker of hope remained. A belief that love, true love, could conquer all. A conviction that she deserved to be happy, even if it meant defying the expectations of others. This flicker, however small, was enough to guide her through the darkness, to propel her forward into the unknown.

Amina rose from the riverbank, her heart heavy but her resolve strengthened. The decision was not yet made, but the contemplation had begun. The exploration of her emotional landscape had revealed the depth of her love for Malik and the extent of her yearning for freedom. And with that knowledge, she took her first step towards an uncertain future.

Malik stood silhouetted against the fiery sunset, the orange hues painting a stark contrast against his usually gentle features. Amina watched him from the shadows of her family's compound, her heart a tangled mess of love and despair. He had come to her, as he always did, under the cloak of darkness, but tonight, the air hung heavy with a different kind of sorrow. He was leaving. Not just for the night, but leaving the village, leaving her world, in a desperate attempt to free her from the chains of tradition that bound her.

He had always been the challenger, the outsider, the one who questioned the ancient ways. But now, his rebellion took a different form – a selfless act of love. He knew that their stolen moments, their whispered promises under the watchful eyes of the stars, were no longer enough. The noose of her arranged marriage was tightening, and he couldn't bear to watch her be forced into a life devoid of love, a life where her spirit would slowly wither and die.

"I cannot stay here and watch you become someone else's wife, Amina," he said, his voice rough with emotion. "It would break me. Every sunrise would be a reminder of what we could have had, of what you deserve." His words were like shards of glass, piercing her heart, yet she understood. She understood the depth of his love, a love so profound that it compelled him to walk away, to sacrifice his own happiness for her sake.

He wasn't running away from his feelings, but rather running towards a solution, however improbable it seemed. He envisioned a life for them, a life where they could be together without the suffocating weight of tradition, a life where their love could blossom freely, unburdened by the expectations of others. He would go to the city, find work, build a foundation, and then, only then, would he dare to hope that she would follow.

Amina knew the city was a distant dream, a place whispered about in hushed tones, a place where the old ways were slowly fading. It represented freedom, opportunity, but also uncertainty and danger. The thought of leaving her family, her community, the only world she had ever known, was terrifying. Yet, the thought of living without Malik, of spending her days with a man she did not love, was an even greater terror.

Malik saw the turmoil in her eyes, the battle raging within her soul. He reached out, his calloused hand gently cupping her face. "I know this is not easy, Amina. I know I am asking you to leave everything behind. But I also know that you are strong, that you are capable of making your own choices. Your heart knows the truth, and you must listen to it."

He wasn't demanding, wasn't pressuring her. He was simply offering her a choice, a chance at a life filled with love and authenticity. He was laying bare his own vulnerability, revealing the depth of his commitment to her happiness. He was willing to endure the pain of separation, the uncertainty of the future, all for the possibility that one day, they would be together, truly together.

His selflessness was a beacon in the darkness, a testament to the power of his love. He wasn't just thinking of himself, of his own desires. He was thinking of her, of her well-being, of her right to choose her own destiny. He was willing to relinquish his own happiness if it meant that she could find hers, even if that happiness didn't include him.

In that moment, Amina saw Malik not just as her lover, but as her savior, her champion, the one person who truly believed in her, who saw beyond the expectations and traditions that threatened to consume her. His love was a fire, burning bright and unwavering, a fire that gave her the courage to question, to challenge, to dream of a different future.

As he prepared to leave, he pressed a small, intricately carved wooden bird into her hand. "A reminder," he whispered, "that even caged birds can learn to fly. That even when surrounded by walls, the spirit can soar." He turned and disappeared into the night, leaving Amina alone with her thoughts, her fears, and the burning ember of hope that Malik had ignited within her heart. The decision was hers, and hers alone. The weight of it settled upon her shoulders, heavy and daunting, but also strangely empowering. She had a choice, and that, in itself, was a victory.

CHAPTER: 6

WEDDING BELLS OR CHAINS?

The drums throbbed, a relentless heartbeat echoing the frantic rhythm in Amina's chest. Each beat was a hammer blow, forging the chains that bound her to a destiny not of her choosing. The vibrant colors of the wedding celebrations blurred into a suffocating kaleidoscope, the joyous ululations of the women sounding like mournful cries in her ears. She walked, or rather, was propelled forward by the invisible force of tradition, her feet heavy, her spirit leaden.

The weight of the *gele*, the elaborate headscarf, pressed down on her, a physical manifestation of the expectations crushing her soul. It was her grandmother, Jamila, who had painstakingly tied it, her wrinkled hands trembling slightly as she secured each fold. Amina remembered the warmth of Jamila's touch, the silent plea in her eyes – a plea for Amina to be strong, to honor her family, to accept her fate. But how could she, when her heart yearned for something more, something real?

Kwame awaited her at the end of the aisle, a figure of imposing strength and quiet dignity. He was everything her family wanted in a husband – respected, wealthy, and deeply rooted in the community. He wore a traditional *agbada*, the flowing robe embroidered with intricate patterns, a symbol of his status and lineage. He stood tall, his gaze unwavering, radiating an aura of confidence and certainty. But in Amina's eyes, there was no spark, no flicker of recognition, only a polite, almost distant, acknowledgement.

She tried to focus on the familiar faces in the crowd – her mother, her aunts, her cousins – all beaming with pride and approval. But their smiles felt like masks, concealing the disappointment that would surely follow if she dared to deviate from the script that had been written for her. Only Jabulani, her uncle, offered a subtle nod of encouragement, a silent acknowledgment of the turmoil raging within her. His eyes held a knowing sadness, a shared understanding of the price of tradition.

The air grew thick with the scent of incense and the sweet aroma of traditional delicacies, but Amina's appetite had vanished. Her stomach churned with a mixture of anxiety and rebellion. She felt like a puppet, her strings pulled taut by the expectations of her family and the weight of her culture. Each step she took was a betrayal of her own heart, a surrender to a life that was not truly hers.

As she drew closer to Kwame, she could feel the heat radiating from his body, the anticipation simmering beneath his composed exterior. He reached out his hand, his touch firm and possessive. Amina hesitated, her fingers trembling as she placed her hand in his. The contact sent a jolt through her, a chilling reminder of the commitment she was about to make – a commitment that would bind her to him for life.

The priest began to speak, his voice booming through the courtyard, reciting the ancient vows that had been spoken for generations. Amina listened, her mind racing, her heart pounding. The words echoed in her ears, each syllable a nail hammered into the coffin of her dreams. She glanced at Kwame, his face etched with a serene contentment, oblivious to the storm brewing within her.

She thought of Malik, his eyes filled with a passionate fire, his touch sending shivers down her spine. She remembered their secret meetings, their stolen kisses, their whispered promises of a future together. He was everything Kwame was not – an outsider, a rebel, a man who challenged the status quo. But he was also the man she loved, the man who made her feel alive, the man who saw her for who she truly was.

A wave of nausea washed over her, and she swayed slightly, her vision blurring. The faces in the crowd swam before her eyes, their expressions morphing into grotesque caricatures of disapproval and judgment. She felt trapped, suffocated, as if the walls of the courtyard were closing in on her, crushing her beneath their weight.

The priest continued to speak, his voice droning on, oblivious to the internal battle raging within Amina. He asked for her consent, his eyes fixed on her expectantly. The silence stretched, thick and heavy, as all eyes turned to her, waiting for her response. Amina opened her mouth to speak, but no words came out. Her throat was dry, her voice trapped within her chest.

She looked at Kwame again, his face now etched with a hint of concern. He squeezed her hand gently, a silent reassurance. But his touch felt like a cage, trapping her within the confines of his expectations. She closed her eyes, took a deep breath, and braced herself for the inevitable. She was about to say the words that would seal her fate, the words that would bind her to a life she did not want.

But then, a commotion erupted at the back of the courtyard. A gasp rippled through the crowd, heads turned, and a collective murmur arose. Amina opened her eyes, her heart leaping with a mixture of hope and dread. She knew, instinctively, who it was. Malik had come. He had come to disrupt her wedding, to challenge her fate, to fight for her love. The drums stopped, the priest fell silent, and all eyes turned to the figure striding purposefully towards them, his face a mask of determination.

Malik's arrival was like a thunderclap, shattering the carefully constructed facade of tradition and order. He moved with a fierce urgency, his eyes fixed on Amina, his presence radiating a raw, untamed energy that sent shivers down her spine. He was a whirlwind of defiance, a force of nature that threatened to uproot everything in its path. The carefully orchestrated ceremony teetered on the brink of chaos, the air thick with anticipation and uncertainty.

Kwame's hand tightened around Amina's, his face hardening with anger and resentment. He knew, in that instant, that his carefully laid plans were about to unravel, that the woman he had believed would be his wife was about to be stolen away from him. The seeds of bitterness and revenge began to sprout within him, poisoning his heart and clouding his judgment. The stage was set for a confrontation, a battle between love and duty, between tradition and freedom, between Kwame and Malik.

Amina stood frozen, caught between two worlds, two destinies. Her heart pounded in her chest, her mind reeling with confusion and conflicting emotions. She knew that whatever decision she made in that moment would have profound and lasting consequences, not only for herself but for her family, her community, and the man she loved. The weight of her decision pressed down on her, threatening to crush her beneath its immensity. The wedding bells had become chains, binding her to a fate she could no longer accept.

The drums, which had been a steady, rhythmic heartbeat throughout the morning, faltered, skipped a beat, then resumed, a little faster, a little more frantic. Amina barely registered the change. Her world had narrowed to the path before her, the feel of the heavy, embroidered cloth of her wedding dress dragging against her skin, the scent of incense and nervous sweat clinging to the air.

Each step was a monumental effort, a battle against the screaming voice inside her that begged her to turn, to run, to disappear into the familiar embrace of the hills that cradled their village. But tradition, duty, and the weight of her family's expectations held her captive, each invisible chain binding her tighter with every step she took towards Kwame.

She could see him now, standing at the head of the aisle, a proud, imposing figure in his own traditional attire. His face was set in an expression she couldn't quite decipher – anticipation? Triumph? Or something else, something colder, that sent a shiver down her spine despite the sweltering heat.

Her gaze flickered to her parents, their faces etched with pride and satisfaction. They believed they were doing what was best for her, securing her future, solidifying their family's standing in the community. They couldn't possibly understand the hollowness that echoed within her, the gaping void where joy should have been.

As she drew closer, the murmurs of the crowd intensified, a low hum of expectation that pressed in on her from all sides. She felt like a lamb being led to slaughter, a sacrifice to the gods of tradition and obligation. Her heart hammered against her ribs, a desperate bird trapped in a cage.

Suddenly, a ripple of commotion spread through the crowd. Heads turned, whispers erupted, and the rhythmic drumming faltered once more, this time threatening to dissolve into complete silence. Amina's breath caught in her throat. What was happening?

Then, she saw him. Malik. Standing at the edge of the courtyard, a lone figure silhouetted against the bright sunlight. He looked different, bolder, more determined than she had ever seen him. Gone was the hesitant, almost apologetic air he usually carried in the face of societal disapproval. He stood tall, his eyes locked on hers, a silent plea etched on his face.

A collective gasp swept through the crowd. The audacity! The sheer defiance of his presence was a slap in the face to everything they held sacred. Mansa, her grandfather, visibly stiffened, his face darkening with fury. Her father's hand tightened on her arm, his grip almost painful.

Malik took a step forward, then another, his voice cutting through the stunned silence. "Amina!" he called out, his voice raw with emotion. "Don't do this. Don't sacrifice your happiness for a life you don't want."

The words hung in the air, a challenge to the very foundations of their society. Amina's heart leaped in her chest. Hope, a dangerous, forbidden emotion, flickered within her. She looked from Malik to Kwame, from her parents to her grandfather, their faces a mixture of shock, anger, and disbelief.

"Choose love, Amina," Malik continued, his voice growing stronger, more impassioned. "Choose your heart. Don't let tradition chain you to a life of unhappiness. I know it's not easy, but I also know the strength you possess. I know you can make this decision."

His words were a lifeline, a beacon in the darkness that threatened to engulf her. She saw the truth in his eyes, the unwavering belief in her ability to choose her own destiny. But the fear was still there, the fear of disappointing her family, of being ostracized, of losing everything she had ever known.

Kwame's face was a mask of fury. He took a step towards Malik, his fists clenched. "How dare you!" he roared. "This is my wedding day! You have no right to interfere."

But Malik stood his ground, his eyes never leaving Amina's. "She has the right to choose," he said, his voice firm. "She has the right to love."

The drums fell silent. The air crackled with tension. All eyes were on Amina, the weight of their expectations pressing down on her, threatening to crush her. The crossroads had arrived, and the decision was hers alone. Would she choose the well-worn path of tradition, or would she dare to forge her own way, a path paved with love and uncertainty?

The drums, which had moments ago pulsed with the joyous rhythm of celebration, seemed to falter, their beat mirroring the sudden tremor in Amina's heart. The vibrant colors of the wedding party, the swirling fabrics of the dancers, the beaming faces of her family — all blurred into a kaleidoscope of expectation, each element a weight pressing down on her, suffocating her spirit. She could feel the eyes of the entire village upon her, each gaze a silent demand, a reminder of the traditions she was bound to uphold.

Kwame stood at the altar, a figure of quiet strength and unwavering faith. His eyes, usually filled with warmth and affection, held a flicker of uncertainty, a shadow of doubt that mirrored her own. He was a good man, a respected member of the community, a partner who would provide her with security and stability. He represented everything her family wanted for her, everything she had been raised to believe was right. But as she looked at him, she felt a hollowness in her chest, a void that no amount of societal approval could fill.

Then, a ripple of murmurs spread through the crowd, a collective gasp that stole the air from her lungs. Heads turned, eyes widened, and a path seemed to open as if by divine intervention. There, standing at the edge of the courtyard, was Malik. His presence was a stark contrast to the vibrant colors of the wedding, a dark silhouette against the joyous backdrop. He was an outsider, a challenger to the traditions that bound her, a symbol of the life she yearned for but dared not imagine.

His eyes met hers, and in that instant, the world around her faded away. The drums, the dancers, the faces of her family – all vanished, leaving only the raw, undeniable connection that existed between them. His gaze was a plea, a silent invitation to break free from the chains of duty and embrace the freedom of her own heart. It was a dangerous invitation, one that could shatter her family, disgrace her community, and condemn her to a life of exile. But it was also an invitation to true love, to a life lived on her own terms, a life filled with passion and purpose.

Malik's voice, though soft, carried through the stunned silence, each word a hammer blow against the foundation of tradition. He spoke of their shared dreams, of their unwavering love, of the life they could build together, a life free from the constraints of expectation. His words were a challenge to the elders, a defiance of the customs that had dictated their lives for generations. They were a declaration of war against the forces that sought to keep them apart.

Amina's heart pounded in her chest, a frantic drumbeat urging her to choose. Her mind raced, weighing the consequences of her decision. On one side lay the security of tradition, the comfort of familiarity, the approval of her family. On the other side lay the uncertainty of freedom, the risk of exile, the promise of true love. It was an impossible choice, a Sophie's Choice of the heart, and the weight of it threatened to crush her.

The air crackled with anticipation, every breath held, every eye fixed upon her. The elders, their faces etched with disapproval, stood as silent sentinels of tradition, their presence a formidable barrier against her desires. Her mother, her eyes filled with a mixture of hope and fear, watched her with a silent plea, begging her to choose wisely, to protect the family's honor, to secure her own future.

Kwame, his face a mask of stoic resolve, stood at the altar, waiting. He deserved her respect, her loyalty, her commitment. He had done nothing to warrant this humiliation, this public display of defiance. Yet, as she looked at him, she knew that she could not marry him, not when her heart belonged to another, not when her soul yearned for a different path.

Zuri, her younger cousin, stood at the edge of the crowd, her eyes shining with admiration and a hint of envy. She had always admired Amina's strength, her independence, her willingness to challenge the status quo. In this moment, Amina was not just choosing her own destiny, she was paving the way for Zuri and the other young women of the village to question the traditions that bound them, to dream of a future where they could choose their own paths.

Amina closed her eyes, took a deep breath, and whispered a silent prayer. She asked for guidance, for strength, for the courage to follow her heart, no matter the cost. When she opened her eyes, her gaze was clear, her resolve unwavering. She knew what she had to do, what she had to say. The tension in the air was palpable, a thick, suffocating blanket that threatened to smother her. But beneath that tension, a spark of hope flickered, a promise of change, a possibility of a new beginning.

The weight of generations, the expectations of her family, the traditions of her village – all pressed down on her, threatening to suffocate her spirit. But within her, a fire burned, a fierce, unyielding flame that refused to be extinguished. It was the fire of love, the fire of freedom, the fire of her own indomitable will. And in that moment, she knew that she could not, would not, let it be quenched.

She stood at the crossroads of her life, a solitary figure against the backdrop of tradition, facing an impossible decision. The fate of her family, the future of her community, and the destiny of her own heart hung in the balance. The world held its breath, waiting for her to speak, waiting for her to choose. And in the silence that followed, Amina knew that her life would never be the same again.

The wedding day was not merely a union of two individuals; it was a tapestry woven with the threads of generations, a vibrant display of the village's soul. Every aspect, from the rhythmic drumming to the intricate beadwork on the bride's attire, held deep cultural significance. It was a day when the past, present, and future converged, a testament to the enduring traditions that bound the community together.

For Amina, however, the weight of these traditions felt like an unbearable burden. The vibrant colors of her isidwaba, the traditional wedding dress, seemed to mock her inner turmoil. The rhythmic chants of the women, usually a source of comfort and joy, now echoed her entrapment. She was a lamb being led to the altar, a sacrifice to the gods of custom and expectation.

The expectations placed upon the bride were immense, a culmination of years of cultural conditioning. She was expected to be obedient, respectful, and above all, fertile. Her primary role was to bear children, especially sons, to carry on the family name and legacy. Her personal desires, her dreams, her very essence, were secondary to this sacred duty.

Amina knew these expectations intimately. She had grown up hearing stories of women who had dutifully fulfilled their roles, sacrificing their own happiness for the sake of their families. She had witnessed the quiet resignation in their eyes, the unspoken longing for a life unlived. And she had vowed, deep within her heart, that she would not suffer the same fate.

The wedding ceremony itself was a complex ritual, a series of symbolic acts designed to unite the bride and groom and their respective families. The exchange of gifts, the sharing of food, the blessings from the elders – each element carried a profound meaning, reinforcing the bonds of kinship and community. The lobola, or bride price, had already been negotiated, a testament to the value placed upon the bride and her potential to contribute to her new family.

As Amina walked towards Kwame, she saw not the man she was about to marry, but the embodiment of these expectations. He was a symbol of tradition, of duty, of a life preordained. He was a kind and honorable man, she knew, but he was not the man her heart yearned for. He was not Malik.

The drums beat louder, the chants grew more fervent, and the air crackled with anticipation. Amina felt as though she were drowning in a sea of expectations, her voice lost in the cacophony of tradition. She longed to break free, to scream, to run, but her feet were rooted to the ground, held captive by the invisible chains of duty.

She glanced at her mother, her eyes filled with a mixture of pride and concern. Her mother had also been a bride, many years ago, and had dutifully fulfilled her role as wife and mother. Amina knew that her mother loved her, but she also knew that her mother believed in the sanctity of tradition. To defy it would be to betray everything her mother held dear.

And then she saw him. Malik. Standing at the edge of the crowd, his eyes filled with a desperate plea. He was a beacon of hope in the darkness, a reminder that there was another path, a path of love and freedom. His presence was a challenge, a provocation, a promise of a life beyond the confines of tradition.

In that moment, Amina knew that she could not go through with it. She could not sacrifice her happiness, her dreams, her very soul, for the sake of tradition. She had to choose. She had to choose between duty and love, between obedience and freedom, between the life that was expected of her and the life that she yearned to live.

The weight of the world seemed to rest upon her shoulders as she stood at the crossroads of her life, the wedding bells tolling like a death knell, each chime a reminder of the chains that bound her. The decision she was about to make would not only change her life, but would also send ripples throughout the village, challenging the very foundations of their traditions.

The cultural significance of the wedding was undeniable, a cornerstone of their society. But Amina had come to realize that tradition should not be a prison, but a guide. It should not dictate one's destiny, but rather inform it. And she was determined to forge her own destiny, even if it meant defying the expectations of her family and her community.

The air grew thick with anticipation, the silence broken only by the pounding of Amina's heart and the distant call of a lone bird. All eyes were on her, waiting, watching, judging. She was the center of attention, the focal point of a drama that had been centuries in the making. And she was about to rewrite the script.

Kwame stood tall and proud, a beacon of tradition in his meticulously chosen attire. The rich fabric, woven with symbols of his lineage and status, felt comforting against his skin. Today was the day he would finally take Amina as his wife, a union that would solidify his family's standing and bring honor to their name. He had always envisioned this day, a day of celebration, unity, and the beginning of a prosperous future.

He had prepared himself, not just with the finest clothes and gifts, but also with a heart full of anticipation. He believed in the sanctity of marriage, a sacred bond ordained by God and upheld by their ancestors. To him, it was more than just a union of two individuals; it was a covenant, a promise to build a life together based on mutual respect, shared values, and unwavering commitment.

Kwame had watched Amina from afar for many years, admiring her beauty, her grace, and her quiet strength. He saw in her a woman who would be a devoted wife, a loving mother, and a pillar of their community. He knew that their marriage was arranged, but he also believed that love could blossom even in the most carefully planned unions. He was determined to earn her affection, to prove himself worthy of her hand, and to build a marriage that would be the envy of all.

As he made his way to the ceremony, Kwame greeted the elders with respect, his heart swelling with pride. He saw the approving nods, the smiles of encouragement, and the knowing glances that spoke of a shared understanding of the importance of this day. He was fulfilling his duty, not just to his family, but to his community, to his ancestors, and to God.

He imagined Amina walking towards him, radiant in her bridal attire, her eyes sparkling with happiness. He pictured himself taking her hand, vowing to love and cherish her for all eternity. He dreamt of building a home filled with laughter, children, and the warmth of their shared love.

Kwame had spent countless hours preparing for this day, ensuring that every detail was perfect. He had consulted with the elders, sought their blessings, and followed every tradition with meticulous care. He wanted to show Amina and her family that he was a man of honor, a man of his word, and a man who would always put their needs before his own.

He understood the weight of his responsibilities, the expectations placed upon him as a husband and a leader. He was ready to embrace those responsibilities, to guide his family with wisdom, to protect them from harm, and to provide them with a life of comfort and security.

Kwame's unwavering belief in the sanctity of marriage was not merely a cultural obligation; it was a deeply held conviction that resonated with his faith. He had prayed for guidance, sought divine blessings, and trusted that God had orchestrated this union for a greater purpose. He was confident that with faith as their foundation, their marriage would withstand any storm and flourish for generations to come.

He thought of the future, of the children they would raise, instilling in them the values of their ancestors, the importance of faith, and the strength of family bonds. He envisioned a legacy of love, respect, and unwavering commitment that would inspire generations to come.

As he approached the wedding venue, Kwame paused, taking a deep breath, his heart pounding with anticipation. He could hear the music, the laughter, and the murmur of the crowd. He knew that Amina was waiting for him, ready to begin their new life together. He straightened his shoulders, adjusted his attire, and stepped forward, ready to embrace his destiny.

He imagined their first dance, a slow, graceful waltz that would symbolize their unity and their shared journey. He pictured their first home, a cozy haven filled with warmth and love. He dreamt of their first child, a precious gift that would bind them together forever.

Kwame's anticipation was not just about the wedding day; it was about the lifetime of love and companionship that lay ahead. He was ready to embark on this journey with Amina, to face whatever challenges may come their way, and to build a life that was both fulfilling and meaningful.

He had no doubt that their marriage would be a success, a testament to the power of tradition, the strength of faith, and the enduring bond of family. He was ready to be a husband, a father, and a leader, to fulfill his destiny and to make his family proud.

With a confident stride and a hopeful heart, Kwame entered the wedding venue, ready to claim his bride and begin their new chapter together, completely unaware of the turmoil brewing in Amina's heart and the disruption that was about to unfold.

CHAPTER: 7

BETRAYAL & CONSEQUENCES

The air crackled with anticipation, thick with the scent of incense and the rhythmic pulse of drums. Amina stood before the assembled families, the vibrant colors of her wedding attire suddenly feeling like a suffocating shroud. Kwame, his face beaming with pride, stood beside her, a symbol of tradition and the embodiment of her family's expectations. But in her heart, a different name echoed, a different face haunted her dreams – Malik.

The moment had arrived, the question poised to seal her fate. The elder, his voice resonating with the weight of generations, intoned the sacred words, asking for her assent. Amina's breath hitched in her throat, her gaze darting to the shadows where she knew, she just knew, Malik was watching. His presence, though unseen by most, was a tangible force, a silent plea that resonated with the deepest desires of her soul.

Amina closed her eyes, a whirlwind of memories crashing over her – stolen moments with Malik under the ancient baobab tree, whispered promises beneath the starlit sky, the intoxicating feeling of true love blossoming in a world determined to keep them apart. But then, the faces of her family swam into focus – her mother's gentle smile, her father's stoic pride, her grandmother's knowing eyes. The weight of their expectations, the burden of tradition, threatened to crush her.

But as she looked at Kwame, she saw not a loving partner, but a gilded cage. A life of duty, devoid of passion, stretched before her like a barren wasteland. The thought of spending her days with a man she did not love, of bearing children in a loveless union, filled her with a profound sense of despair. It was a betrayal of herself, a denial of the very essence of her being.

Amina opened her eyes, her gaze hardening with newfound resolve. The drums seemed to fade into the background, the scent of incense no longer intoxicating but cloying. She took a deep breath, the air filling her lungs with a strength she didn't know she possessed. Her voice, when it came, was clear and unwavering, cutting through the expectant silence like a sharp blade.

"I cannot," she declared, the words echoing through the stunned assembly. A collective gasp rippled through the crowd, faces contorting in disbelief and outrage. Kwame's smile faltered, his eyes widening in confusion and hurt. Her mother's face crumpled, tears welling in her eyes. Her father's jaw tightened, his expression hardening into a mask of fury.

"I cannot marry Kwame," Amina continued, her voice gaining strength with each word. "My heart belongs to another. I cannot live a lie, a life devoid of love. I will not sacrifice my happiness for the sake of tradition."

The silence that followed was deafening, broken only by the soft sobs of her mother and the ragged breathing of her father. The elder stared at her, his face a mask of disbelief, his eyes burning with disapproval. Kwame stood frozen, his pride shattered, his dreams crumbling before his eyes.

Amina's act of defiance was a seismic event, a shattering of the established order. It was a rebellion against the very foundations of their society, a challenge to the authority of the elders and the sanctity of tradition. It was a declaration that love, true love, was worth more than obedience, more than duty, more than the expectations of others.

But in that moment of liberation, Amina also knew that she had unleashed a storm. She had betrayed her family, defied her community, and shattered the dreams of a man who had done nothing to deserve such humiliation. The consequences of her actions would be far-reaching, and she braced herself for the fallout, knowing that her life would never be the same again.

The whispers started immediately, a low hum of shock and disapproval that quickly escalated into a cacophony of outrage. Fingers pointed, heads shook, and angry murmurs filled the air. Amina stood tall, her chin held high, but inside, her heart trembled with fear and uncertainty. She had chosen love, but at what cost?

Kwame, recovering from his initial shock, stared at Amina with a mixture of hurt and anger. The humiliation was evident in his eyes, the sting of rejection a palpable presence. He had been publicly scorned, his pride wounded, and his future irrevocably altered. The weight of tradition, once a source of strength, now felt like a crushing burden.

The carefully orchestrated ceremony, meant to solidify family ties and ensure a prosperous future, had devolved into a scene of chaos and disgrace. Amina's act of defiance had not only shattered her own life but had also sent shockwaves through the entire community, threatening to unravel the very fabric of their society.

The silence that followed Amina's pronouncement was thick, suffocating. It pressed down on her, heavier than any expectation, any tradition. The vibrant colors of the wedding attire seemed to dim, the joyous ululations of the women fading into a distant hum. All eyes were on Mansa, the patriarch, the unwavering pillar of their family and community. His face, usually etched with the wisdom of generations, was now a mask of thunderous disbelief.

Amina watched him, her heart pounding against her ribs, each beat a painful reminder of the love she was sacrificing, the family she was potentially losing. She had known this moment would be fraught with peril, but the sheer force of Mansa's reaction threatened to shatter her resolve. She had hoped, perhaps naively, that her grandfather, a man she had always revered, would see the truth in her heart, the undeniable love that bound her to Malik.

But tradition, like a deeply rooted tree, held Mansa in its unyielding grip. He had always been a staunch defender of their customs, a guardian of their heritage. To him, Amina's defiance was not just a personal choice; it was an affront to their ancestors, a betrayal of everything they held sacred. The whispers began, hushed at first, then growing in volume, a chorus of disapproval that echoed through the courtyard.

Mansa stood tall, his gaze unwavering, his voice resonating with a power that silenced the murmurs. "Amina," he began, his voice laced with a chilling disappointment, "you have brought shame upon this family. You have spat upon the traditions that have sustained us for generations. You have chosen your own selfish desires over the honor of your lineage."

Tears welled in Amina's eyes, blurring her vision, but she refused to look away. She would not cower, would not shrink from the consequences of her choice. This was her life, her heart, and she would not let tradition dictate her fate. "Grandfather," she pleaded, her voice trembling but firm, "I did not intend to bring dishonor. But I cannot marry Kwame. My heart belongs to another."

Mansa's eyes narrowed, his face hardening with each word. "Your heart?" he scoffed. "Your heart is a foolish thing, easily swayed by fleeting desires. Duty, Amina, duty is what matters. Family is what matters. You have forsaken both."

He paused, his gaze sweeping over the assembled guests, his voice ringing with authority. "Let it be known," he declared, "that Amina is no longer a daughter of this house. She has severed her ties to this family, to this community. She is dead to us."

The words hung in the air, heavy and final. Amina gasped, a sharp pain piercing her chest. Disowned. Cast out. The weight of Mansa's pronouncement crashed down on her, crushing her spirit. She had anticipated rejection, but this... this was a death sentence. To be banished from her family, from her home, was to lose a part of herself, a part she could never reclaim.

Jamila, her grandmother, stepped forward, her face etched with sorrow. She reached out to Amina, her hand trembling. "Mansa, please," she begged, her voice barely a whisper. "Don't do this. She is still your granddaughter."

Mansa turned to Jamila, his eyes softening for a moment, but then hardening again. "She made her choice, Jamila," he said, his voice firm. "She must face the consequences."

He turned back to Amina, his gaze cold and unforgiving. "From this day forward," he said, his voice ringing with finality, "you are no longer welcome in this home. Your name will not be spoken. You are dead to us."

With those words, Mansa turned and walked away, his back ramrod straight, his shoulders squared. The crowd parted before him, their faces a mixture of shock, disapproval, and pity. Amina stood alone, the weight of her grandfather's rejection crushing her spirit. She had chosen love, but at what cost? Had she truly sacrificed everything for a fleeting dream?

The vibrant colors of her wedding attire now seemed like a cruel mockery, the joyous ululations replaced by a deafening silence. She was alone, adrift in a sea of disapproval, cast out from the only home she had ever known. The future stretched before her, uncertain and daunting. But amidst the pain and despair, a flicker of defiance ignited within her. She would not be broken. She would not be defined by her grandfather's rejection. She would forge her own path, create her own family, and prove that love, true love, was worth fighting for, even if it meant defying tradition and facing the consequences alone.

As Mansa walked away, the weight of his decision settled upon him. He knew he had acted harshly, but he believed he had done what was necessary to protect his family's honor. Yet, a nagging doubt lingered in his mind. Had he been too rigid? Too unforgiving? Was tradition worth sacrificing the happiness of his own granddaughter? Only time would tell if he had made the right choice, or if his actions would ultimately tear his family apart.

The air in the village, once thick with the sweet anticipation of a wedding, now hung heavy with a palpable tension. Amina's defiant act, her refusal to marry Kwame before the assembled families and elders, had sent shockwaves rippling through the community. It was as if a stone had been thrown into a still pond, the ripples disturbing the placid surface of tradition and custom.

Whispers followed Amina's name like shadows. Women, who had once admired her quiet grace, now averted their gaze, their faces etched with disapproval. Men, who had respected her family's standing, now muttered about the disgrace she had brought upon them. The very ground she walked on seemed to vibrate with the collective judgment of the village.

The marketplace, usually a vibrant tapestry of sounds and colors, felt muted, subdued. Amina, who once enjoyed bartering for fresh produce and sharing laughter with her friends, now found herself an outcast. The familiar faces of vendors and neighbors turned away, their smiles replaced with cold indifference. The sense of community, once a source of comfort and belonging, now felt like a suffocating weight.

Children, too, felt the shift in the atmosphere. They no longer ran to greet Amina with playful shouts, their innocent eyes now reflecting the disapproval they had absorbed from their parents. The games they played seemed to lack their usual joy, the laughter replaced with a nervous silence.

Even the church, a sanctuary of solace and spiritual guidance, offered no refuge. The whispers followed Amina even within its hallowed walls, the disapproving glances of fellow parishioners piercing her soul. The comforting words of the sermon seemed to mock her, the message of obedience and duty resonating with a painful irony.

The elders, the custodians of tradition and the arbiters of social order, convened in hushed tones, their faces grim with concern. Amina's act of defiance was not merely a personal transgression; it was a challenge to the very foundation of their society, a threat to the carefully constructed edifice of customs and expectations.

The consequences extended beyond mere social ostracism. Amina's family, once respected and admired, now faced ridicule and shame. Their standing in the community diminished, their influence waned, and their future prospects seemed uncertain. The weight of Amina's actions threatened to crush them all.

Jabulani, Amina's progressive uncle, found himself caught in a precarious position. While he sympathized with Amina's desire for personal freedom, he also understood the importance of maintaining social harmony. He attempted to mediate between Amina and the elders, but his efforts were met with resistance and suspicion.

Zuri, Amina's younger cousin, watched the unfolding drama with a mixture of fear and admiration. She saw the pain and isolation Amina endured, but she also recognized the courage and conviction that fueled her defiance. Amina's actions sparked a flicker of rebellion within Zuri's own heart, a questioning of the traditions she had always taken for granted.

Kwame, the rejected suitor, felt the sting of humiliation and the burning embers of anger. His pride wounded, his reputation tarnished, he struggled to comprehend Amina's rejection. He had been raised to believe that marriage was a matter of duty and honor, not of personal choice. Amina's actions challenged his deeply held beliefs, leaving him confused and resentful.

Even Malik, the object of Amina's affection, felt the weight of the consequences. He knew that their love had ignited this firestorm, and he bore the responsibility for the pain and suffering it had caused. He questioned whether their love was worth the price, whether their happiness could ever justify the disruption they had wrought.

The village, once a symbol of unity and tradition, now stood divided, fractured by Amina's act of defiance. The consequences of her actions reverberated through every aspect of their lives, casting a long shadow over their future. The question that hung heavy in the air was whether they could ever heal the wounds and restore the harmony that had been shattered.

The air in the village, once thick with the sweet anticipation of a wedding, now hung heavy with a palpable sense of condemnation. Amina's defiance wasn't merely a personal choice; it was a seismic tremor that threatened to destabilize the very foundations upon which their community was built. The elders, the keepers of tradition, whispered amongst themselves, their faces etched with a mixture of disbelief and disapproval. The younger generation, however, watched with a mixture of fear and fascination, their hearts stirring with a nascent understanding of the courage it took to challenge the status quo.

The immediate repercussion was Amina's isolation. Women who had once shared secrets and laughter with her now averted their gaze, their silence a deafening indictment. The marketplace, once a vibrant tapestry of social interaction, became a gauntlet of judgment, each glance a sharp reminder of her transgression. Even the children, who had once clamored for her attention, now shied away, their innocent faces reflecting the prejudice they had absorbed from their parents.

The cultural implications were profound. In a society where marriage was not merely a union of individuals but a strategic alliance between families, Amina's refusal was seen as an act of betrayal, a rejection of the collective wisdom of generations. The lobola, the bride price that had been painstakingly negotiated, now seemed like a mockery, a symbol of a contract broken and a promise unfulfilled. The ancestors, whose spirits were believed to watch over the village, were said to be displeased, their blessings withdrawn from a community that had dared to defy their ancient customs.

The social repercussions extended beyond mere ostracism. Amina's actions cast a shadow of doubt on the suitability of other young women for marriage. Families became wary of allowing their daughters too much freedom, fearing that they too might be swayed by the allure of personal desire over familial duty. The village became a pressure cooker of suppressed emotions and unspoken anxieties, the once harmonious rhythm of life disrupted by the discordant note of Amina's rebellion.

Even Zuri, Amina's confidante, found herself facing the consequences of her association with the disgraced bride-to-be. Whispers followed her through the village, casting doubt on her own character and intentions. Her parents, anxious to protect her reputation, restricted her movements and forbade her from speaking to Amina, fearing that her rebellious spirit might be contagious.

The church, once a source of solace and guidance, became a battleground of conflicting interpretations. Some members condemned Amina's actions as a violation of God's will, citing scriptures that emphasized obedience and submission. Others, however, saw her defiance as an act of faith, a courageous stand for the sanctity of love and the freedom of choice. The pastor, caught in the crossfire of these opposing views, struggled to reconcile the demands of tradition with the tenets of his faith.

Malik, too, faced his share of repercussions. As an outsider, he had always been viewed with suspicion, his self-made success seen as a challenge to the established social order. Now, he was branded as a troublemaker, a seducer who had lured Amina away from her rightful path. His business suffered, his customers dwindling as they distanced themselves from the man who had dared to defy the village's customs.

The weight of the community's disapproval pressed down on Amina, threatening to suffocate her spirit. She found herself questioning her decision, wondering if the price of her freedom was too high. The faces of her family, etched with disappointment and anger, haunted her dreams, their silent accusations more painful than any words could convey.

Yet, amidst the darkness, a flicker of hope remained. Jabulani, her progressive uncle, continued to offer her quiet support, reminding her that she was not alone in her struggle. He spoke of the need for change, of the importance of questioning outdated traditions and embracing a more compassionate and inclusive vision of community.

And Amina herself, despite the pain and isolation, refused to be broken. She clung to her faith, drawing strength from the belief that God had a purpose for her, a reason for leading her down this difficult path. She resolved to prove to her family and her community that love and tradition could coexist, that it was possible to honor the past while forging a new future.

Amina's defiance, therefore, became a catalyst for change, a spark that ignited a debate about the true meaning of tradition, the limits of obedience, and the power of love to transcend even the most deeply ingrained cultural norms. The village, once a bastion of unwavering conformity, was now a community grappling with its own identity, its future hanging in the balance, dependent on whether it could find a way to reconcile the demands of the past with the aspirations of the present.

The whispers grew louder, the stares more piercing, but Amina walked with her head held high, knowing that she had chosen the path of her heart, a path that, though fraught with challenges, was ultimately leading her towards a future where love, faith, and freedom could finally intertwine.

Mansa stood as a monument to tradition, unyielding and resolute in his beliefs. His face, a roadmap of wrinkles etched by years of unwavering adherence to ancestral customs, was set in a permanent scowl. Amina's defiance was not merely a personal affront; it was an earthquake that threatened to topple the very foundations upon which his life, his family, and his community were built.

For Mansa, tradition was not a set of dusty relics to be admired from afar; it was the lifeblood that coursed through the veins of their people. It was the compass that guided their steps, the shield that protected them from the chaos of the outside world. To deviate from it was to invite disaster, to unravel the intricate tapestry woven by generations of ancestors.

He had always envisioned Amina as a vessel of continuity, a link in the unbroken chain that stretched back to the very origins of their tribe. Her marriage to Kwame was not simply a union of two individuals; it was a strategic alliance, a reaffirmation of their family's status and influence within the community. It was a duty, a sacred obligation that she was now so carelessly discarding.

In Mansa's eyes, Amina's love for Malik was a frivolous infatuation, a fleeting fancy that paled in comparison to the weight of tradition. He saw Malik as an outsider, a threat to the established order, a man who dared to challenge the wisdom of the elders. He could not fathom how Amina could prioritize her own desires over the well-being of her family and her community.

He remembered the countless hours he had spent imparting the wisdom of their ancestors to Amina, instilling in her the values of obedience, sacrifice, and duty. He had hoped that she would grow into a woman who understood the importance of upholding tradition, a woman who would embrace her role in preserving their cultural heritage. But now, it seemed that his efforts had been in vain.

As he watched Amina stand before him, defiant and unrepentant, Mansa felt a surge of anger and disappointment. He could not comprehend her choices, her motivations, her blatant disregard for the traditions that had shaped their lives. He saw her not as his granddaughter, but as a traitor, a rebel who had betrayed her family and her community.

His inability to accept Amina's choices stemmed from a deep-seated fear of change. He believed that any deviation from tradition would lead to the erosion of their cultural identity, the disintegration of their social fabric. He clung to the past with an iron grip, unwilling to acknowledge the possibility that progress and tradition could coexist.

Mansa's world was one of absolutes, of right and wrong, of black and white. There was no room for nuance, no space for compromise. Amina's actions had shattered his rigid worldview, leaving him feeling lost and disoriented. He could not reconcile her defiance with the image he had always held of her, the obedient and dutiful granddaughter he had raised.

The whispers of the village elders fueled his resolve. They saw Amina's actions as a sign of the times, a symptom of the growing influence of the outside world on their traditional way of life. They urged Mansa to take a firm stance, to send a clear message that such defiance would not be tolerated.

And so, Mansa hardened his heart, steeling himself against the pleas of his family and the whispers of his conscience. He saw himself as a guardian of tradition, a protector of their cultural heritage. He would not allow Amina's rebellion to undermine the values that had sustained their community for generations.

He would disown her, sever all ties with her, and cast her out into the wilderness. It was a harsh decision, a painful sacrifice, but one that he believed was necessary to preserve the integrity of their traditions. He would show her, and the rest of the village, that the consequences of defying tradition were severe and unforgiving.

In his heart, a small voice whispered a plea for understanding, a flicker of doubt that questioned the righteousness of his actions. But Mansa quickly silenced it, burying it beneath layers of pride, duty, and fear. He could not afford to waver, to show any sign of weakness. The fate of his family, his community, and his traditions rested on his shoulders.

As he turned his back on Amina, Mansa felt a pang of regret, a fleeting moment of sadness for the granddaughter he was losing. But he knew that he could not allow his personal feelings to cloud his judgment. He had a duty to uphold, a tradition to protect. And he would do whatever it took, even if it meant sacrificing the love of his own family.

His unwavering adherence to tradition, his inability to accept Amina's choices, would ultimately define him, shaping his legacy and casting a long shadow over the lives of those he loved. He was a man of his time, a product of his culture, a prisoner of his own beliefs. And in the end, he would choose tradition over love, duty over compassion, and the past over the future.

CHAPTER: 8

EXILE & SURVIVAL

The dust swirled around their feet as they fled, each grain a tiny reminder of the life Amina was leaving behind. The vibrant colors of her village, the familiar scent of her mother's cooking, the comforting rhythm of daily life – all fading into a distant memory as they journeyed further away. With Malik's hand clasped tightly in hers, Amina pressed forward, her heart a tumultuous mix of fear and hope. The weight of her family's condemnation was a heavy burden, yet the promise of a life lived on her own terms propelled her onward.

Their destination was a city she had only heard whispers of – a place where traditions held less sway, where individuals carved their own paths, and where anonymity offered a shield from prying eyes and wagging tongues. It was a gamble, a leap of faith into the unknown, but Amina knew she could not remain in the village, suffocated by the expectations and judgments that had defined her existence. The memory of her grandfather's face, contorted with rage and disappointment, haunted her, but she refused to let it break her spirit.

The journey was arduous, the landscape unforgiving. They traveled by foot and by crowded, rickety buses, each mile a testament to their determination. Malik, ever the protector, shielded her from the harsh realities of their flight, his unwavering love a beacon in the darkness. He shared stories of the city, painting a picture of opportunity and freedom, but Amina knew that the reality might be far different from his hopeful vision.

As they approached the city limits, the air grew thick with anticipation. The skyline was a chaotic jumble of buildings, a stark contrast to the serene beauty of her village. The noise was deafening, the crowds overwhelming, and the sheer scale of it all left Amina feeling both exhilarated and terrified. This was a world unlike anything she had ever known, a place where she would have to forge a new identity and build a new life from scratch.

The initial days were a blur of disorientation and uncertainty. They found a small, cramped room in a rundown neighborhood, a far cry from the spacious compound she had grown up in. The city was a melting pot of cultures and languages, and Amina struggled to find her footing in this unfamiliar environment. She missed the familiar faces of her friends and family, the comforting rituals of her faith, and the sense of belonging that had always grounded her.

Malik, resourceful and determined, quickly found work as a laborer, his strong hands and unwavering work ethic earning him the respect of his colleagues. He worked tirelessly to provide for them, his love for Amina evident in every sacrifice he made. But Amina knew that their survival depended on more than just his hard work. She needed to find her own purpose, her own way to contribute to their new life.

The weight of her decision began to settle upon her, a heavy cloak of regret and self-doubt. Had she been foolish to abandon her family, her community, her entire way of life for the sake of love? Was she strong enough to withstand the challenges that lay ahead? The whispers of her conscience echoed in her mind, questioning her choices and fueling her anxieties.

Sleep offered little respite, her dreams haunted by visions of her village, her family, and the life she had left behind. She saw her mother's tear-streaked face, her grandfather's disapproving gaze, and the empty space where she once belonged. The guilt gnawed at her, threatening to consume her entirely.

In her darkest moments, she turned to her faith, seeking solace and guidance in the familiar words of the scriptures. She prayed for strength, for wisdom, and for the courage to face whatever the future held. Her faith was a lifeline, a reminder that she was not alone, that God was with her, even in this unfamiliar and uncertain place.

As the days turned into weeks, Amina began to find her own rhythm in the city. She explored the bustling marketplaces, marveling at the vibrant colors and exotic aromas. She met other women who had left their villages in search of a better life, women who understood her struggles and offered her support. She started taking classes at a local community center, learning new skills and expanding her horizons.

Slowly, tentatively, Amina began to build a new identity, one that was rooted in her past but open to the possibilities of the future. She was no longer just Amina, the dutiful daughter of a traditional family. She was Amina, a woman of strength, resilience, and unwavering faith, determined to create a life of her own choosing.

The city, once a daunting and overwhelming place, began to feel like home. It was not the home she had known, but a new kind of home, one built on love, freedom, and the courage to defy expectations. The journey ahead would not be easy, but Amina knew that she was not alone. She had Malik by her side, her faith in her heart, and the unwavering belief that she could overcome any obstacle that stood in her way.

The city was a stark contrast to the village Amina had always known. Gone were the familiar faces, the comforting rhythm of daily life, and the unwavering support of her community. Here, anonymity reigned, and Amina felt like a tiny boat adrift on a vast, unforgiving ocean.

The initial excitement of freedom had begun to wane, replaced by a gnawing sense of isolation. She missed her mother's gentle touch, her grandmother's wise counsel, and even the playful banter with Zuri. The weight of her decision pressed heavily on her shoulders, a constant reminder of the family she had left behind.

Days bled into weeks, and the unfamiliarity of their surroundings began to take its toll. The bustling marketplace, once a source of fascination, now felt overwhelming. The faces of strangers blurred into a sea of indifference, offering no solace or connection.

Amina found herself spending hours gazing out of their small apartment window, her thoughts drifting back to the village. She pictured her family gathered around the evening fire, sharing stories and laughter. A pang of longing shot through her heart, a sharp reminder of the joy she had sacrificed.

Regret, like a insidious weed, began to sprout in the fertile ground of her mind. Had she been too hasty in her decision? Had she overestimated her ability to navigate this new life? Doubts gnawed at her, whispering insidious questions that threatened to unravel her resolve.

Malik, ever attentive, noticed the change in her demeanor. He saw the sadness in her eyes, the weariness in her step. He tried to reassure her, reminding her of their love and the promise of a brighter future. But his words, though well-intentioned, often fell short of easing her pain.

One evening, as they sat in silence, Amina confessed her doubts. "Malik," she said, her voice barely above a whisper, "did we do the right thing? Did I make a terrible mistake?"

Malik took her hand, his gaze filled with unwavering love and determination. "Amina," he replied, "we chose love. We chose freedom. It won't be easy, but we will face these challenges together. We will build a new life, a life filled with happiness and purpose."

But even his words couldn't fully dispel the darkness that had settled over her. The weight of her decision was a heavy burden, and she knew that the road ahead would be long and arduous. The whispers of regret continued to haunt her, a constant reminder of the sacrifices she had made.

Amina tried to find solace in her faith, but even prayer offered little comfort. She questioned God's plan for her life, wondering if she had somehow strayed from the path He had intended. The familiar verses of scripture seemed to offer no answers, leaving her feeling lost and alone.

She missed the familiar hymns of the village church, the comforting presence of the elders, and the unwavering faith of her community. Here, in this unfamiliar city, she felt like a stranger in a strange land, cut off from the spiritual nourishment she had always relied upon.

The isolation was compounded by the practical challenges of their new life. Finding work proved difficult, and their meager savings dwindled with each passing day. They struggled to make ends meet, often going without basic necessities.

Amina, who had always been accustomed to a life of relative comfort, found herself facing hardships she had never imagined. She missed the security of her family's home, the abundance of food, and the unwavering support of her community.

Despite the challenges, Amina refused to give up hope. She knew that she had made a difficult choice, but she was determined to make it work. She clung to her love for Malik, her faith in God, and her unwavering belief in a brighter future.

But the road ahead was long and uncertain, and the whispers of regret continued to echo in her heart. Only time would tell if she had made the right decision, or if she would forever be haunted by the family and community she had left behind.

The city was a stark contrast to the village Amina had always known. Buildings scraped the sky, a chaotic symphony of sounds replaced the familiar rhythms of nature, and faces, a kaleidoscope of ethnicities, rushed past without a glance. The anonymity was both a blessing and a curse. It offered a shield from the judging eyes of her community, yet it amplified the gnawing loneliness that had begun to settle deep within her bones.

She and Malik had found a small, sparsely furnished room in a bustling neighborhood, a far cry from the spacious compound she had grown up in. The walls were thin, the air thick with the smells of unfamiliar spices and the constant hum of city life. Every corner of their new dwelling seemed to whisper of their exile, a constant reminder of the life she had left behind.

Malik, ever the optimist, tried to fill their days with hope. He worked tirelessly, taking on odd jobs to make ends meet, his brow often furrowed with worry. He spoke of a future where they could build a life free from the constraints of tradition, a life where their love could blossom without fear.

But Amina couldn't shake the feeling that they were building on shaky ground, a foundation of dreams and uncertainty.

Days bled into weeks, and the initial excitement of freedom began to wane. Amina found herself spending hours staring out the window, watching the city unfold beneath her. She missed the familiar faces of her family, the comforting rituals of her faith, the sense of belonging that had always been a part of her identity. The city offered opportunity, yes, but at what cost?

The weight of her decision pressed down on her, a heavy cloak of regret. Had she been selfish? Had she prioritized her own desires over the well-being of her family? The questions echoed in her mind, relentless and unforgiving. She longed to speak to her grandmother, Jamila, to seek her wisdom and guidance. But the thought of facing her family, of seeing the disappointment in their eyes, was too much to bear.

Her faith, once a source of unwavering strength, now felt like a fragile thread. She prayed, pouring out her doubts and fears, but the answers seemed elusive. The familiar verses of the Bible offered little comfort, the words echoing in the emptiness of her heart. Was she being punished for defying tradition? Had she strayed too far from the path that God had intended for her?

She remembered Jabulani's words, her progressive uncle, before she left the village. 'A marriage without love is a house without a foundation.' But what if the foundation she had chosen was built on sand? What if, in her pursuit of love, she had inadvertently destroyed the very fabric of her being?

One evening, as the city lights twinkled outside their window, Amina confessed her doubts to Malik. Her voice trembled as she spoke of her longing for home, her fear that she had made a terrible mistake. Malik listened patiently, his eyes filled with understanding and compassion. He held her close, offering words of comfort and reassurance.

"We will face this together, Amina," he said, his voice soft but firm. "We will build a new life, a life where love and faith can coexist. It will not be easy, but we will not give up. We will find our way, together."

His words offered a glimmer of hope, a reminder that she was not alone in this journey. But the questions lingered, a persistent undercurrent of uncertainty. Had she truly made the right choice? Only time would tell if their love could withstand the test of exile, if their faith could guide them through the darkness. For now, all she could do was hold on to hope, and pray for guidance as she navigated the unfamiliar terrain of her new life.

The city, a sprawling mass of unfamiliar faces and towering buildings, was a stark contrast to the close-knit village Amina had always known. Gone were the familiar greetings, the comforting rhythm of daily life, and the unwavering support of her community. Here, she was just another face in the crowd, anonymous and alone.

The initial excitement of freedom quickly faded, replaced by the harsh realities of survival. Malik, ever the provider, secured work as a laborer, his strong hands calloused and weary from long hours under the relentless sun. Amina, however, struggled to find her footing. Her skills, honed in the village, were of little use in this urban landscape. She yearned to contribute, to ease Malik's burden, but opportunities were scarce.

The weight of her decision pressed heavily upon her. Had she been selfish? Had she traded the security of her family for a fleeting dream of love? The questions haunted her waking hours, casting a shadow over her newfound freedom. She missed her grandmother's gentle wisdom, her mother's comforting embrace, even the familiar scolding of her father. The village, with all its constraints, had been her home, her anchor.

Loneliness became her constant companion. She longed for a friendly face, a shared laugh, a moment of connection. The city offered anonymity, but it also demanded isolation. She tried to strike up conversations with her neighbors, but they were wary, guarded. Trust, she realized, was a precious commodity in this unforgiving environment.

Financial struggles added another layer of complexity to their already precarious situation. The cost of living in the city was exorbitant, and Malik's meager wages barely covered their basic needs. They lived in a cramped, dilapidated apartment, a far cry from the spacious compound she had grown up in. Food was scarce, and luxuries were nonexistent.

Amina's faith, once a source of unwavering strength, was now tested like never before. She prayed for guidance, for reassurance, but the silence was deafening. Doubts crept into her mind, whispering insidious questions about her choices and her worthiness. Was she being punished for defying tradition? Had she angered God by choosing love over duty?

The city, with its allure of opportunity and freedom, had become a crucible, testing the very core of her being. She was forced to confront her own limitations, her own vulnerabilities. The sheltered girl from the village was slowly transforming into a resilient woman, forged in the fires of adversity.

One day, while wandering through the bustling marketplace, Amina stumbled upon a small stall selling handcrafted goods. An idea sparked in her mind. She had always been skilled with her hands, creating intricate beadwork and weaving beautiful fabrics. Perhaps she could use these skills to earn a living, to contribute to their survival.

She approached the stall owner, a kind-faced woman named Fatima, and offered to sell her creations. Fatima, impressed by Amina's talent and determination, agreed to give her a chance. With renewed hope, Amina set to work, pouring her heart and soul into each piece.

Slowly but surely, her creations began to attract attention. People were drawn to the vibrant colors, the intricate designs, and the story behind each piece. Amina's work became a symbol of her resilience, her ability to find beauty and hope in the midst of hardship.

As Amina found her place in the city, she also began to find herself. She learned to navigate the complexities of urban life, to stand up for herself, and to embrace her newfound independence. The challenges she faced had not broken her; they had made her stronger, more resourceful, and more determined to create a life of her own choosing.

The city, once a symbol of exile and isolation, was slowly becoming her home. It was a place where she could be herself, where she could pursue her dreams, and where she could build a future with Malik, a future based on love, not tradition.

The initial days in the city were a blur of anxiety and uncertainty, but as the weeks turned into months, Amina and Malik began to find a rhythm in their new life. The shared hardship, the constant need to rely on each other, forged faced the fire of tradition and emerged stronger, more resilient, and more deeply in love than ever before. Their exile had become their liberation, their struggle had become their triumph, and their love had become their testament to the power of choice and the enduring strength of the human spirit.

CHAPTER: 9

SHADOWS OF THE PAST

News of Amina's defiance spread through the village like wildfire, carried on the whispers of the wind and the hushed tones of concerned neighbors. The older generation, those who clung tightly to the threads of tradition, spoke of her actions with a mixture of shock and disapproval. They saw her rebellion as a dangerous crack in the foundation of their carefully constructed society, a threat to the order and stability they had always known.

But among the younger villagers, a different sentiment began to brew. Amina's courage, her willingness to defy the expectations of her family and community, resonated with them in a way that the elders could not understand. They saw in her a glimmer of hope, a possibility that they, too, could break free from the constraints of tradition and forge their own paths in life.

Zuri, Amina's younger cousin, had always been a spirited and independent girl. She loved Amina dearly and admired her strength and intelligence. But she had also felt the weight of tradition, the pressure to conform to the expectations of her family and community. Amina's actions had ignited a spark within her, a desire to question the norms and values she had always taken for granted.

Tyrone, a young man from a humble background, had always felt like an outsider in the village. He was intelligent and ambitious, but he lacked the connections and resources that would allow him to rise above his circumstances. He had always admired Amina's kindness and compassion, and he saw in her a kindred spirit, someone who understood what it was like to feel different and out of place.

Together, Zuri and Tyrone began to question the traditions they had always known. They challenged the elders' assumptions, debated the merits of arranged marriages, and explored the possibility of a different kind of future for themselves and their community. Their conversations were often heated and passionate, but they were always conducted with respect and a genuine desire to understand each other's perspectives.

One evening, as the sun began to dip below the horizon, casting long shadows across the village, Zuri and Tyrone found themselves sitting by the river, lost in thought. The gentle murmur of the water filled the air, creating a sense of peace and tranquility. "Do you think we can really change things?" Zuri asked, her voice barely above a whisper.

Tyrone looked at her, his eyes filled with determination. "I don't know," he said, "but we have to try. Amina showed us that it's possible to stand up for what we believe in, even when it's difficult. We can't just sit back and accept things the way they are. We have to fight for a better future, a future where everyone has the freedom to choose their own destiny."

Zuri nodded, her heart filled with a renewed sense of hope. "You're right," she said. "We can't give up. We have to keep questioning, keep challenging, keep pushing for change. Amina may be gone, but her spirit lives on in us. We have to honor her memory by fighting for the things she believed in."

And so, Zuri and Tyrone embarked on a journey of self-discovery and social activism. They organized meetings, led discussions, and challenged the elders to reconsider their views on tradition and progress. They faced resistance and opposition, but they never wavered in their commitment to creating a more just and equitable society for all.

Their efforts did not go unnoticed. Slowly but surely, other young villagers began to join their cause, inspired by their courage and their unwavering belief in the possibility of change. The seeds of rebellion had been sown, and the village would never be the same again. Amina's sacrifice had not been in vain. Her legacy lived on in the hearts and minds of the younger generation, who were determined to create a future where love and freedom could triumph over tradition and oppression.

The sting of Amina's rejection was a festering wound in Kwame's heart, a humiliation that echoed through the village and reverberated within his very being. He, Kwame, the son of Chief Adebayo, the man destined for greatness, had been publicly scorned. Not just rejected, but replaced, cast aside for an outsider, a man who dared to challenge the traditions that had shaped their lives for generations. The shame was a heavy cloak, suffocating him, and beneath it, a dark seed of vengeance began to sprout.

Sleep offered no escape. Nightmares plagued him, visions of Amina's face, radiant with love, but not for him. He saw Malik's triumphant smirk, a constant reminder of his defeat. Each morning, he awoke with a renewed sense of injustice, the burning desire to reclaim his honor, to make them both pay for the pain they had inflicted.

His first target was Malik. Kwame knew he couldn't simply confront him directly; that would be impulsive, foolish. He needed a plan, a way to dismantle Malik's life piece by piece, to expose him for the outsider he was, to turn the village against him. He started subtly, whispering doubts about Malik's intentions, questioning his motives for staying in the village. He reminded people of Malik's lack of lineage, his disregard for their customs, painting him as a threat to their way of life.

Kwame used his family's influence to his advantage. He spoke to elders, subtly planting seeds of discontent, reminding them of the importance of tradition and the dangers of allowing outsiders to disrupt their harmony. He knew that fear was a powerful weapon, and he wielded it with precision, carefully manipulating the villagers' anxieties.

But his anger wasn't solely directed at Malik. Amina, the woman he had envisioned as his wife, the mother of his children, was equally culpable. He couldn't understand her betrayal, her willingness to abandon everything they had both been raised to believe in. How could she choose a fleeting infatuation over the stability and security of a life within their community? He saw her actions as a personal affront, a deliberate act of defiance against him and his family.

His thoughts turned darker, more insidious. He considered ways to make Amina suffer, to make her regret her decision. He knew that harming her directly would bring shame upon his family, but there were other ways to inflict pain, to make her life as an outcast unbearable. He thought of isolating her from her friends, of spreading rumors to tarnish her reputation, of making her life a living hell.

He confided in no one, not even his closest friends. The weight of his anger was a burden he carried alone, fueling his every action. He became consumed by his quest for revenge, his once-bright eyes now clouded with bitterness and resentment. The village, once a place of comfort and belonging, now felt like a stage for his personal drama, a battleground where he would fight to reclaim his honor.

His mother, sensing the darkness that had enveloped her son, tried to reason with him. She pleaded with him to let go of his anger, to forgive Amina and Malik, to move on with his life. But Kwame was deaf to her pleas. His heart was hardened, his mind set on retribution. He saw himself as a victim, wronged and betrayed, and he would not rest until justice was served.

Kwame's transformation was unsettling. He became withdrawn, secretive, his laughter replaced by a cold, calculating silence. He spent hours alone, plotting and scheming, his mind a labyrinth of vengeful thoughts. Those who had once admired him now regarded him with caution, sensing the storm brewing within him.

The path of revenge was a dangerous one, and Kwame was walking it blindly, unaware of the consequences that awaited him. He was so consumed by his anger that he failed to see the destruction he was causing, not just to Amina and Malik, but to himself. The once-promising young man was now a prisoner of his own bitterness, his future clouded by the shadows of the past.

Amina's defiant act, her bold rejection of the arranged marriage, hung in the air like the scent of woodsmoke after a fire. It had scorched the traditions of the village, leaving behind a landscape forever altered. While the elders grappled with the immediate fallout, a different kind of transformation was brewing amongst the younger generation. Zuri, Amina's younger cousin, found herself at the epicenter of this shift. She had always been a spirited girl, but Amina's courage ignited a flame within her, a yearning to question the unquestionable.

Tyrone, a young man known more for his mischievous grin than his adherence to tradition, was similarly affected. He had witnessed the wedding disruption with wide-eyed astonishment, the seeds of doubt planted in his mind. The rigid expectations that had always seemed immutable now appeared vulnerable, cracked by Amina's rebellion. He found himself drawn to Zuri, and together, they became unlikely catalysts for change.

The marketplace, once a symbol of unwavering tradition, became their informal meeting ground. Under the guise of bartering for goods, they exchanged whispered thoughts and shared forbidden ideas. They spoke of Amina's bravery, her unwavering commitment to her heart, and the possibility of a different kind of future, one where young people had a voice in shaping their own destinies.

Zuri, always the more outspoken of the two, began to challenge the elders in subtle ways. During community gatherings, she would pose questions that, on the surface, seemed innocent enough, but beneath the veneer of respect lay a quiet defiance. She questioned the necessity of certain customs, the fairness of arranged marriages, and the limitations placed upon women. Her words were carefully chosen, designed to provoke thought without inciting outright anger.

Tyrone, in his own way, began to challenge the established order. He started by questioning the traditional roles assigned to young men, the expectation that they should blindly follow in their fathers' footsteps. He spoke of his own dreams, his desire to pursue a different path, one that wasn't dictated by lineage or expectation. His quiet rebellion resonated with other young men who had harbored similar aspirations but lacked the courage to voice them.

Their actions, though seemingly small, had a ripple effect throughout the village. Other young people, emboldened by their example, began to question the traditions they had always known. Secret meetings were held under the cover of darkness, where they discussed their hopes and dreams for the future. They spoke of a village where love was not dictated by tradition, where women had the right to choose their own paths, and where young people had a voice in shaping their own destinies.

The elders, sensing the shift in the wind, grew increasingly uneasy. They saw Amina's rebellion as a dangerous precedent, a threat to the very fabric of their society. They attempted to quell the rising tide of dissent, reminding the young people of their duty to uphold tradition and respect their elders. But their words fell on increasingly deaf ears.

The village, once a bastion of unwavering tradition, was now a battleground between the old and the new. The younger generation, inspired by Amina's courage, was determined to forge a different path, one that honored the past while embracing the future. The elders, clinging to their traditions, were equally determined to maintain the established order.

The conflict between the generations intensified, creating a palpable tension throughout the village. Families were divided, friendships were strained, and the once-harmonious community was now fractured by dissent. The future of the village hung in the balance, dependent on whether the old could adapt to the new, or whether the new would ultimately overthrow the old.

One evening, under the cloak of a star-studded sky, Zuri and Tyrone found themselves by the river, the same river where Amina often sought solace. They gazed at the water, its gentle flow a symbol of the ever-changing nature of life. "Do you think we can really change things?" Tyrone asked, his voice laced with a hint of doubt.

Zuri, her eyes filled with determination, replied, "Amina showed us that it's possible. It won't be easy, but if we stand together, if we remain true to our beliefs, we can create a better future for ourselves and for generations to come." Their words echoed in the night, a testament to the enduring power of hope and the unwavering spirit of youth.

The seeds of change had been sown, and though the path ahead was uncertain, the younger generation of the village was ready to face the challenges that lay ahead. They were the shadows of Amina's past, but they were also the promise of a brighter future, a future where faith and fire could coexist, where blood ties were strengthened by love, and where broken vows could be mended by forgiveness.

The sting of Amina's rejection festered within Kwame, transforming the proud, confident suitor into a vessel of simmering rage. The humiliation he suffered in front of the entire village, the shattering of his carefully constructed future, fueled a burning desire for retribution. He had always been a man of honor, a pillar of the community, and Amina's defiance had not only wounded his pride but had also cast a shadow upon his family's name.

Kwame found himself ostracized, not in the same overt manner as Amina, but in a subtle, insidious way. The whispers followed him, the averted gazes, the hushed conversations that ceased abruptly as he approached. He was no longer the golden boy, the man destined for greatness; he was the jilted groom, the one who had been publicly rejected for an outsider, a man of no consequence.

His anger was a tempestuous storm, raging against Amina, against Malik, and even against the traditions he had always upheld. He questioned the very foundations of his beliefs, wondering if the rigid adherence to custom had blinded him to the desires and needs of the heart. But even in his moments of doubt, the desire for revenge burned brighter, eclipsing any flicker of understanding or empathy.

Kwame's initial impulse was to confront Malik directly, to settle the score with fists and fury. But the elders cautioned him against such rash action, reminding him that violence would only further tarnish his family's reputation. They urged him to seek a more calculated form of retribution, one that would restore his honor and punish Amina and Malik for their transgression.

He began to meticulously plot his revenge, carefully considering every angle, every possible outcome. He knew that he could not simply harm Amina physically; that would only make him a brute, no better than the outsider she had chosen. Instead, he sought to strike at their happiness, to dismantle their newfound life, to make them regret the day they defied tradition.

Kwame started by subtly undermining Malik's reputation, spreading rumors and innuendo about his character and his intentions. He painted Malik as a charlatan, a man who had seduced Amina with false promises and stolen her away from her family. He whispered doubts about Malik's ability to provide for Amina, suggesting that their love was nothing more than a fleeting infatuation that would soon crumble under the weight of reality.

He also turned his attention to Amina's family, subtly manipulating their emotions and fueling their resentment towards her. He reminded them of the shame she had brought upon them, the disgrace she had inflicted upon their ancestors. He played upon their fears and insecurities, suggesting that Amina's rebellion would inspire other young women to defy tradition, leading to the unraveling of their entire way of life.

Kwame's actions were subtle but effective, slowly poisoning the well of goodwill that Amina and Malik had hoped to find in their new life. He knew that he could not completely destroy them, but he could make their existence miserable, a constant reminder of the price they had paid for their defiance.

As Kwame delved deeper into his quest for revenge, he became increasingly consumed by his own bitterness and resentment. He lost sight of the man he once was, the honorable suitor who had been respected and admired by all. He was now a shadow of his former self, driven by a single-minded desire to inflict pain and suffering upon those who had wronged him.

His transformation was a stark reminder of the destructive power of anger and the corrosive effects of revenge. Kwame's journey from heartbroken groom to vengeful adversary was a cautionary tale, a testament to the dangers of allowing bitterness to consume one's soul. The shadows of the past were indeed long, and they threatened to engulf Kwame entirely, leaving him lost in a darkness of his own making.

The village, once a place of familiar comfort, now felt like a stage for Kwame's simmering rage. Every corner held a memory, every face a silent judgment. He was trapped in a cycle of resentment, unable to move forward, his future tethered to the past by the chains of his own making. The proud

Kwame was fading, replaced by a man consumed by the need to settle a score, a man willing to sacrifice his own well-being for the sake of retribution.

Even his family, initially supportive of his pain, began to express concern over his growing obsession. They saw the light dimming in his eyes, the warmth replaced by a cold, calculating glint. They urged him to find peace, to let go of the anger that was eating him alive, but their pleas fell on deaf ears. Kwame was too far gone, too deeply entrenched in his quest for revenge to heed their warnings.

The seed of vengeance had been planted, and it was now bearing bitter fruit, poisoning not only Kwame's life but also the lives of those around him. The shadows of the past had become a suffocating shroud, threatening to extinguish the last embers of hope and compassion within his heart. Kwame's descent into darkness was a tragic consequence of Amina's defiance, a testament to the enduring power of tradition and the devastating price of rebellion.

Amina's defiance, a stone thrown into the still pond of village life, sent ripples far beyond her immediate family. The initial shock and outrage began to morph into something more complex, a simmering unease that threatened to boil over into open conflict. The elders, the staunch keepers of tradition, found themselves facing a challenge to their authority unlike anything they had encountered before. Whispers turned into hushed debates, and the once-unquestioned customs were now being scrutinized under the harsh light of Amina's rebellion.

The most immediate consequence was the disruption of the social order. Marriages, the very foundation of their community, were now viewed with a degree of uncertainty. Young women, witnessing Amina's courage, began to question their own arranged futures. The once-clear path of obedience and duty was now obscured by the tantalizing possibility of choice. This newfound questioning, however, was met with fierce resistance from those who feared the erosion of their way of life.

The economic stability of some families was also threatened. Amina's arranged marriage to Kwame was meant to solidify an alliance between two powerful lineages. With that alliance now shattered, both families faced potential financial repercussions. Business deals were put on hold, and old rivalries resurfaced, adding another layer of tension to the already fraught atmosphere.

The church, a place of solace and unity, became a battleground for differing interpretations of faith. Some argued that Amina's actions were a sin against God and tradition, while others believed that God's love and forgiveness extended to those who dared to follow their hearts. The pastor, a respected figure in the community, found himself struggling to reconcile these opposing viewpoints, knowing that his words could either heal or further divide his congregation.

Adding to the turmoil was the growing divide between the older and younger generations. The elders, clinging to the familiar comfort of tradition, saw Amina's rebellion as a direct threat to their authority and way of life. The younger generation, however, inspired by Amina's courage, began to question the rigid customs that had defined their lives. This generational conflict threatened to tear the village apart, pitting parents against children and creating a chasm that seemed impossible to bridge.

Kwame's humiliation and heartbreak fueled a growing resentment that threatened to spill over into violence. He found himself ostracized by some, pitied by others, and consumed by a burning desire for retribution. His once-clear path to a respected position in the community was now blocked by Amina's actions, and he saw her and Malik as the sole obstacles to his happiness.

Adding fuel to the fire was the arrival of outsiders, drawn to the village by the whispers of rebellion and scandal. Journalists and activists, eager to capitalize on the drama, descended upon the community, further disrupting the delicate balance of village life. Their presence only served to exacerbate the existing tensions, turning the village into a stage for a larger cultural and ideological battle.

Even the weather seemed to reflect the turmoil within the village. A prolonged drought, which had been plaguing the region for months, intensified the sense of hardship and uncertainty. Some saw the drought as a sign of God's displeasure, a punishment for Amina's defiance. Others, however, attributed it to the changing climate and the need for sustainable agricultural practices. Regardless of the cause, the drought added another layer of stress to the already strained community.

The village council, the governing body responsible for maintaining order and resolving disputes, found itself overwhelmed by the sheer number of conflicts and challenges. Accusations flew, tempers flared, and the once-respected council members struggled to maintain control. The very fabric of their society seemed to be unraveling, threatening to plunge the village into chaos.

In the midst of all this turmoil, a small group of villagers, inspired by Amina's courage and guided by their faith, began to work towards reconciliation and healing. They organized community meetings, facilitated dialogues between opposing factions, and sought to find common ground amidst the chaos. Their efforts, however, were met with resistance from those who clung to their anger and resentment, making the path to peace a long and arduous one.

One of the most significant challenges was the growing fear of violence. Kwame's simmering anger, coupled with the arrival of outsiders and the breakdown of social order, created a volatile atmosphere. Rumors of planned attacks and retaliatory actions spread like wildfire, further fueling the sense of unease and uncertainty. The villagers, once united by their shared traditions and values, now found themselves living in fear of one another.

The elders, desperate to regain control, resorted to increasingly drastic measures. They imposed stricter rules and regulations, cracked down on dissent, and sought to silence those who dared to question their authority. These actions, however, only served to further alienate the younger generation and exacerbate the existing tensions. The village, once a symbol of unity and harmony, was now a powder keg waiting to explode.

As the village grappled with these new conflicts and challenges, one thing became clear: Amina's rebellion had irrevocably changed the community. The old ways were no longer sufficient to address the complexities of modern life, and the villagers were forced to confront the need for change and adaptation. Whether they would be able to overcome their differences and forge a new path forward remained to be seen, but one thing was certain:

the shadows of the past would continue to haunt them until they found a way to reconcile tradition with the demands of the present.

CHAPTER: 10

A MOTHER'S PLEA

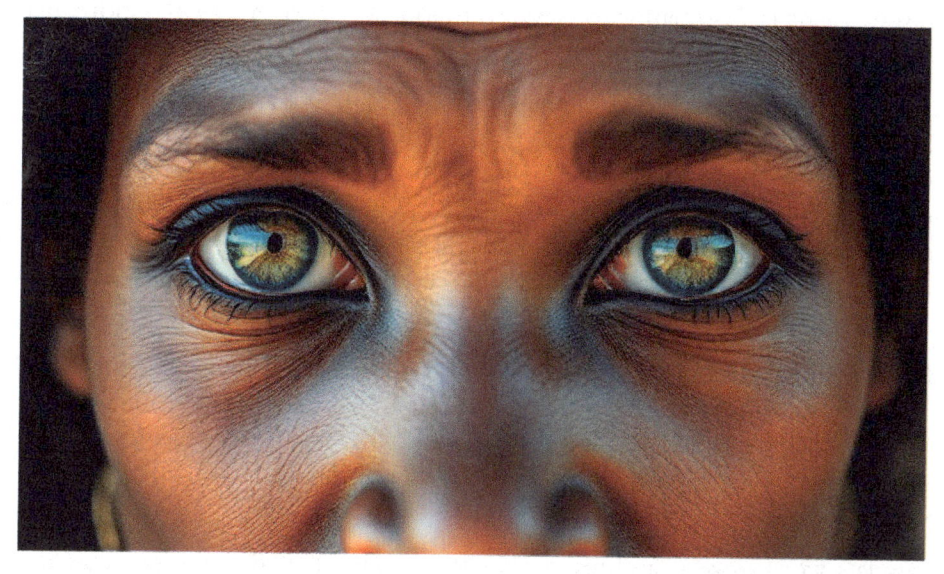

The air in the ancestral home hung thick with unspoken accusations and simmering resentment. Amina's exile had cast a long shadow, chilling the very heart of the family. Mansa, his face etched with disappointment and anger, sat like a stone idol, unyielding in his judgment. The younger generation, Zuri and Tyrone, fidgeted nervously, their eyes darting between the elders, sensing the immense weight of the decision that hung in the balance.

It was Jamila, Amina's grandmother, who finally broke the oppressive silence. Her voice, though aged, carried a strength that resonated through the room. She rose slowly, her movements deliberate, her gaze sweeping across the faces of her family, a plea etched in every line of her weathered face. "My children," she began, her voice trembling slightly, "we are tearing ourselves apart. Is this what we have become? A family consumed by pride and blinded by tradition?"

Her words hung in the air, a challenge to the rigid adherence to customs that had defined their lives for generations. "We speak of honor," she continued, her voice gaining strength, "but where is the honor in casting out our own blood? Where is the honor in denying love and forgiveness? Amina is not a disgrace; she is a woman who dared to follow her heart. And is that not what we all secretly yearn to do?"

Tears welled in Jamila's eyes as she spoke of Amina's childhood, of her bright spirit and her unwavering love for her family. She reminded them of the countless sacrifices Amina had made, of her dedication to upholding their traditions, until her own happiness was at stake. "Have we forgotten the meaning of love?" she implored, her voice filled with sorrow. "Love is not about blind obedience; it is about understanding, compassion, and forgiveness."

She turned to Mansa, her eyes filled with a mixture of love and challenge. "Mansa, my son," she said softly, "I know you believe you are protecting our family's honor, but at what cost? Are you willing to sacrifice your granddaughter's happiness for the sake of tradition? Is that truly the legacy you wish to leave behind?"

Jamila's words struck a chord within the hearts of many present. Jabulani, Amina's progressive uncle, nodded in agreement, his eyes filled with admiration for Jamila's courage. Even some of the more conservative members of the family shifted uncomfortably, their faces reflecting a flicker of doubt.

Kwame, who had been silent throughout the proceedings, watched Jamila with a mixture of resentment and grudging respect. He had come seeking justice, seeking to restore his wounded pride, but Jamila's words forced him to confront the deeper questions at play. Was revenge truly the answer? Would it bring him the peace he so desperately craved?

Jamila's plea was not just for Amina's sake, but for the sake of the entire family. She knew that the rift between them could not heal unless they were willing to embrace forgiveness and understanding. She knew that tradition, while important, should not come at the expense of love and compassion.

She extended her hand towards Mansa, her eyes pleading with him to reconsider his judgment. "Mansa," she said softly, "let us not allow pride and anger to destroy our family. Let us open our hearts to Amina and welcome her back with love and forgiveness. Only then can we truly heal and move forward."

The room remained silent, the weight of Jamila's words hanging heavy in the air. All eyes were on Mansa, waiting for his response. The fate of Amina, and perhaps the future of the family, rested on his decision. Would he soften his heart and embrace forgiveness, or would he remain steadfast in his adherence to tradition, condemning Amina to a life of exile and regret?

The tension was palpable as Mansa stared into the distance, his face unreadable. The weight of generations of tradition pressed down on him, urging him to uphold the customs that had defined their family for centuries. But Jamila's words had planted a seed of doubt in his heart, a flicker of hope that perhaps there was another way, a way to honor tradition without sacrificing love and compassion.

The silence stretched on, each second feeling like an eternity. The fate of Amina, the future of the family, hung precariously in the balance, dependent on the decision of the family patriarch. The power of love and forgiveness, embodied in Jamila's unwavering plea, stood as the only beacon of hope in the face of deeply entrenched tradition.

The air in the grand compound was thick with unspoken accusations and simmering resentment. Amina's exile had cast a long shadow, dimming the once vibrant atmosphere of the family home. While Kwame wrestled with his bruised pride and Zuri and Tyrone grappled with their burgeoning doubts about tradition, Jamila, the family matriarch, felt the weight of their fractured unity most keenly. She watched as Mansa, her son, hardened his heart, clinging to the rigid customs that had always defined their family. But Jamila knew that true strength lay not in unyielding adherence to the past, but in the capacity to adapt, to forgive, and to love.

With a resolve that belied her age, Jamila decided to intervene. She summoned the family, gathering them in the courtyard where Amina's pre-marriage ceremony had once been filled with such hopeful anticipation. Now, the space felt haunted by the ghost of shattered expectations. Jamila stood before them, her eyes filled with a mixture of sorrow and determination. Her voice, though aged, carried the weight of generations, demanding their attention and respect.

"My children," she began, her gaze sweeping across their faces, "we are a family bound by blood and tradition. But what is blood without love? What is tradition without compassion? We have allowed anger and pride to cloud our judgment, to tear us apart. We have forgotten the very essence of what it means to be a family."

Mansa shifted uncomfortably, his jaw tightening. "Mother," he interjected, his voice laced with impatience, "Amina has brought shame upon our family. She has defied our traditions, our ancestors. How can we simply forgive such an act?"

Jamila turned to face her son, her eyes filled with a gentle but unwavering strength. "Mansa," she said, her voice softening, "I understand your anger, your sense of betrayal. But I also see the pain in your eyes, the emptiness in your heart. You cling to tradition as if it were a shield, protecting you from the uncertainties of the world. But tradition should not be a cage, imprisoning our spirits and stifling our capacity for love."

She stepped closer to Mansa, her hand reaching out to gently touch his arm. "Have you truly considered what Amina's happiness means? Have you asked yourself if forcing her into a loveless marriage would truly honor our family? Or would it simply perpetuate a cycle of unhappiness and resentment?"

Her words hung in the air, heavy with unspoken truths. The other family members stirred, their faces reflecting a mixture of surprise and contemplation. Jabulani, Amina's progressive uncle, nodded in agreement, his eyes filled with a glimmer of hope. Even Kwame, his heart still aching from Amina's rejection, seemed to soften slightly, his gaze shifting from the ground to meet Jamila's.

"Mansa," Jamila continued, her voice filled with a quiet urgency, "I have lived a long life, and I have seen much joy and much sorrow. And I have learned that love is the most precious gift we can give and receive. It is the foundation upon which families are built, the force that binds us together in times of hardship. Do not let pride and tradition blind you to the power of love. Do not let Amina's happiness be sacrificed on the altar of outdated customs."

She paused, her gaze sweeping across the faces of her family, her voice filled with a plea that resonated deep within their souls. "Think of Amina, of her spirit, of her dreams. Is it truly worth sacrificing her happiness for the sake of upholding a tradition that no longer serves us? Is it worth losing a daughter, a sister, a granddaughter, for the sake of pride?"

Jamila's words were a balm to the wounded spirits that had gathered in the courtyard. She had spoken not of condemnation, but of understanding; not of judgment, but of forgiveness; not of tradition as an unyielding force, but of love as the ultimate guiding principle. Her plea was a challenge to Mansa's rigid adherence to the past, an invitation to open his heart to the possibility of reconciliation and to consider, for the first time, the true meaning of family.

The air in the homestead hung thick with unspoken words, a heavy silence that threatened to suffocate any hope of reconciliation. Amina's defiance had not only shattered the carefully constructed image of their family but had also exposed the fault lines that had long been hidden beneath the veneer of tradition. Jamila, the matriarch, felt the weight of generations pressing down on her, the echoes of ancestors whispering their disapproval. Yet, within her heart, a fierce love for her granddaughter burned brighter than any societal expectation.

She understood the importance of family bonds, the intricate web of connections that held their community together. But she also recognized the potential for those bonds to become chains, restricting individual growth and stifling the very essence of love. She had witnessed firsthand the pain and suffering caused by forced unions, the silent sacrifices made in the name of duty. And she refused to let Amina become another casualty of tradition.

"Mansa," Jamila began, her voice soft yet firm, cutting through the oppressive silence. "We are a family, bound by blood and history. But what is blood without love? What is history without compassion? We cannot allow tradition to blind us to the needs of our own children." Her gaze swept across the faces of her family, each etched with a mixture of anger, confusion, and pain. She saw the hurt in Kwame's eyes, the bewilderment in her son's, and the unwavering resolve in Mansa's. But she also saw the flicker of doubt, the subtle cracks in their unwavering adherence to tradition.

"Amina has made her choice," Jamila continued, "a choice that has undoubtedly brought shame upon our family. But is shame greater than the love that binds us? Is tradition more important than the happiness of our own flesh and blood? We have always prided ourselves on our strength, our resilience. But true strength lies not in rigid adherence to the past, but in the ability to adapt, to forgive, to embrace the future with open hearts."

She recounted stories of their ancestors, tales of love and loss, of sacrifice and redemption. She reminded them of the times when their family had faced adversity, when they had chosen compassion over judgment, and when they had emerged stronger as a result. She spoke of the power of forgiveness, the ability to heal wounds and mend broken relationships. She emphasized that reconciliation was not a sign of weakness but a testament to their unwavering love for one another.

"We are not perfect," Jamila admitted, "we have made mistakes in the past, and we will undoubtedly make more in the future. But we must learn from those mistakes, grow from them, and strive to create a better future for our children. We cannot allow anger and resentment to consume us, to tear our family apart. We must choose love, choose forgiveness, choose reconciliation."

Her words hung in the air, a beacon of hope in the midst of despair. Some family members remained unmoved, their hearts hardened by tradition and pride. But others began to soften, their eyes reflecting a glimmer of understanding. Kwame, his face etched with pain, looked at Jamila with a mixture of gratitude and confusion. He had always respected her wisdom, but he struggled to reconcile her words with the deep-seated anger he felt towards Amina and Malik.

Even Mansa, the unwavering patriarch, seemed to waver, his gaze softening as he looked at his beloved granddaughter. He had always believed in the importance of tradition, in upholding the values of their ancestors. But he also loved Amina deeply, and he could not bear the thought of losing her forever.

Jamila's plea was not a demand for unconditional acceptance, but a call for understanding, for empathy, for a willingness to bridge the gap that had formed between them. She knew that reconciliation would not be easy, that it would require sacrifice and compromise from all involved. But she also believed that it was possible, that the bonds of family were strong enough to withstand even the most devastating of betrayals.

As the days turned into weeks, Jamila continued to work tirelessly to mend the broken ties within her family. She spoke with each member individually, listening to their concerns, offering her wisdom, and gently guiding them towards forgiveness. She reminded them of the importance of unity, of the strength they derived from their shared history and heritage. Slowly, painstakingly, the seeds of reconciliation began to sprout, nurtured by Jamila's unwavering love and her unwavering belief in the power of family.

The journey was far from over, but the first steps had been taken. The path to healing was long and arduous, but the possibility of redemption loomed on the horizon. And as the family began to tentatively reach out to one another, a glimmer of hope emerged, a promise of a future where tradition and love could coexist, where family bonds could be strengthened rather than broken by the choices of the heart.

Jamila, the matriarch of the family, had always been a beacon of quiet strength and unwavering love. Her face, etched with the stories of generations past, held a depth of wisdom that transcended the rigid customs of their village. Unlike Mansa, who clung to tradition with an iron grip, Jamila understood that true strength lay not in unyielding adherence to the past, but in the ability to adapt, to forgive, and to embrace the ever-changing currents of life.

Her hands, gnarled with age, had soothed countless tears, guided hesitant steps, and offered silent comfort in times of despair. They were hands that had birthed children, tended to the sick, and woven the very fabric of their family together. Now, those same hands trembled slightly as she prepared to speak, knowing that her words could either mend the fractured bonds of her family or shatter them beyond repair.

Jamila's wisdom wasn't born of books or formal education, but from a life lived fully, with all its joys and sorrows. She had witnessed firsthand the destructive power of pride and the transformative magic of forgiveness. She had seen how rigid adherence to tradition could stifle the human spirit, while love, in its purest form, could blossom even in the most barren of landscapes.

She remembered her own youth, a time when she too had felt the constraints of tradition, the pressure to conform to expectations that didn't align with her heart's desires. But she had found a way to navigate those challenges, to carve out a space for herself within the boundaries of their culture, and to instill in her children and grandchildren the importance of both honoring their heritage and pursuing their own paths.

Now, as she looked upon her family, torn apart by Amina's defiance, her heart ached. She saw the pain in Mansa's eyes, the humiliation he felt at being publicly challenged. But she also saw the anguish in Amina's, the desperate plea for understanding and acceptance. And she knew that if anyone could bridge the chasm that had formed between them, it was she.

Jamila had always possessed an uncanny ability to see beyond the surface, to perceive the hidden emotions and unspoken needs that lay beneath the veneer of tradition and expectation. She understood that Mansa's rigidity stemmed from a deep-seated fear of losing control, of seeing the traditions that had defined their family for generations crumble before his eyes.

But she also knew that Amina's rebellion wasn't born of disrespect or malice, but from a genuine desire to live a life of authenticity and love. She saw in Amina a reflection of her own youthful spirit, a yearning for freedom that she herself had once felt so keenly.

And so, as she prepared to speak, Jamila drew upon the wellspring of wisdom that had sustained her through the years. She would not condemn Mansa for his adherence to tradition, nor would she chastise Amina for her defiance. Instead, she would offer a different perspective, a reminder of the values that truly mattered: love, compassion, and forgiveness.

Her unwavering belief in the power of love wasn't a naive sentimentality, but a profound understanding of its transformative potential. She knew that love could heal wounds, mend broken hearts, and bridge even the widest of divides. It was the foundation upon which their family had been built, and it was the only thing that could save them now.

Jamila's love was a quiet, steady flame, burning brightly even in the darkest of times. It was a love that embraced both tradition and progress, that honored the past while looking towards the future. It was a love that saw the potential for good in everyone, even those who seemed lost in anger and resentment.

As she rose to her feet, her frail frame belied the strength of her spirit. Her eyes, though clouded with age, sparkled with an inner light, a testament to the enduring power of love and wisdom. She was the heart of their family, the keeper of their traditions, and the voice of reason that could guide them back from the brink of destruction.

She was Jamila, the matriarch, the peacemaker, and the unwavering believer in the power of love to conquer all. And in this moment of crisis, her family would need her more than ever before.

Jamila's presence commanded respect, not through fear, but through the sheer weight of her experience and the palpable aura of love that surrounded her. Her every movement was deliberate, each word carefully chosen, reflecting a lifetime of thoughtful contemplation and compassionate understanding. She was a living embodiment of the values she preached, a testament to the enduring power of kindness and forgiveness.

Her unwavering belief in love wasn't just a platitude; it was a deeply held conviction, forged in the crucible of life's challenges. She had seen love mend broken hearts, heal fractured relationships, and transform enemies into friends. She knew that it wasn't always easy, that it required sacrifice, patience, and a willingness to see beyond one's own hurt, but she also knew that it was the only path to true and lasting peace.

The air in the homestead hung heavy, thick with unspoken accusations and the lingering scent of the aborted wedding feast. Amina's act had not only disrupted a sacred tradition but had also seemingly poisoned the very well of family unity. Exile and recrimination had become the order of the day, yet amidst this storm of anger and disappointment, a lone voice dared to speak of a different path – the path of forgiveness.

Jamila, the family matriarch, a woman whose life had been a tapestry woven with threads of both joy and sorrow, stepped forward. Her face, etched with the wisdom of years, held a gentle strength that commanded attention. She had witnessed generations rise and fall, seen traditions upheld and challenged, and understood the delicate balance between honoring the past and embracing the future. Now, she saw her family teetering on the brink of irreparable fracture, and her heart ached with a profound sadness.

"My children," she began, her voice resonating with a quiet authority that hushed the murmurs of dissent. "We stand here today, wounded and divided. Anger and pride have blinded us, leading us down a path of bitterness and resentment. But I ask you, what good will come of this? Will holding onto our anger bring Amina back? Will it restore the honor we believe she has tarnished? Or will it simply leave us with nothing but empty hearts and broken bonds?"

Her gaze swept across the faces of her family, lingering on Mansa, his face a mask of rigid disapproval, and then on the younger generation, their eyes filled with confusion and uncertainty. She saw the pain in Kwame's eyes, the sting of rejection and humiliation, but she also saw the flicker of understanding, the nascent recognition that perhaps, there was more to this situation than met the eye.

"Tradition is important," Jamila continued, her voice softening, "It is the foundation upon which we have built our lives, the compass that guides us through the storms of life. But tradition should not be a cage that imprisons our hearts, a chain that binds us to a past that no longer serves us. We must be willing to adapt, to evolve, to find new ways of honoring our heritage while embracing the changing world around us."

She paused, her eyes meeting Mansa's, a silent plea passing between them. "Mansa, my son, I know your heart is heavy with disappointment. You believe that Amina has brought shame upon our family, that she has defied our ancestors and betrayed our trust. But I ask you, is there no room in your heart for forgiveness? Is there no possibility for redemption?"

The word hung in the air, a fragile seed of hope planted in the barren landscape of resentment. Forgiveness. It was a concept that seemed foreign, almost impossible, in the face of such blatant defiance. But Jamila's words had struck a chord, a reminder of the values that lay at the heart of their faith and their community – compassion, understanding, and the unwavering belief in the power of second chances.

The possibility of redemption, too, was introduced, not as a guaranteed outcome, but as a potential path forward. Could Amina, who had dared to defy tradition, ever be welcomed back into the fold? Could Kwame, whose pride had been wounded, find it in his heart to forgive? Could Mansa, the staunch guardian of tradition, learn to embrace a new way of thinking?

These questions lingered, unanswered, but the mere fact that they had been raised was a victory in itself. Jamila's plea had opened a door, a crack in the wall of resentment, allowing a sliver of light to penetrate the darkness. The journey towards forgiveness and redemption would be long and arduous, fraught with challenges and setbacks. But it was a journey worth undertaking, for it held the promise of healing, reconciliation, and the restoration of family unity.

The seed of forgiveness had been planted. Whether it would take root and blossom into a flower of reconciliation remained to be seen. The family, still reeling from Amina's actions, stood at a crossroads, the weight of tradition pulling them in one direction, while the whisper of love and forgiveness beckoned them towards another. The choice, ultimately, was theirs.

CHAPTER: 11

A FAMILY DIVIDED

The humiliation Kwame suffered at the wedding festered within him, a wound that refused to heal. Amina's public rejection wasn't just a personal blow; it was a blatant disregard for the traditions he held sacred, a slap in the face to his family's honor. The whispers followed him everywhere, the pitying glances of villagers fueling his rage. He had been the chosen one, the respected suitor, and now he was the laughingstock, the man publicly scorned.

His pride, once a shield of confidence, now felt like a fragile mask, threatening to shatter with the slightest tremor. He tried to reason with himself, to understand Amina's defiance, but the traditions ingrained in him since childhood clouded his judgment. Love, in his world, was secondary to duty, to the preservation of family ties and ancestral customs. Amina's actions were not just a rejection of him but a rejection of everything he believed in.

The anger simmered beneath the surface, threatening to boil over. He started avoiding the marketplace, the church, any place where he might encounter the knowing eyes of the villagers. Sleep offered no respite, his dreams haunted by Amina's face, by the image of her walking away with Malik. The whispers turned into accusations in his mind, fueling his resentment and driving him to the brink.

It was Jabulani, Amina's progressive uncle, who first noticed the change in Kwame. The once-proud young man was now withdrawn, his eyes filled with a dark intensity. Jabulani, despite his own unconventional views, understood the weight of tradition, the sting of public shame. He tried to reason with Kwame, to offer a different perspective, but his words fell on deaf ears.

"Kwame," Jabulani said, placing a hand on his shoulder, "Amina has made her choice, and while it may not be the one we expected, it is hers to make. Harboring anger will only poison your heart. Find peace, find forgiveness."

Kwame shrugged off Jabulani's hand, his eyes hardening. "Forgiveness? She has disgraced my family, humiliated me in front of the entire village! There is no forgiveness for such a transgression."

Jabulani sighed, knowing he couldn't reach Kwame in his current state. "Then I fear you are on a dangerous path, Kwame. A path that will lead to nothing but pain and destruction."

The warning went unheeded. Kwame's anger continued to fester, fueled by the whispers, the pity, and the unwavering belief that Amina and Malik had wronged him. He began to see Malik as the sole cause of his misery, the interloper who had stolen what was rightfully his. The thought of revenge consumed him, a dark seed taking root in his soul.

One evening, fueled by palm wine and resentment, Kwame confronted Malik on the outskirts of the village. The air crackled with tension as they faced each other, two men bound by Amina's love and divided by tradition and rage.

"You have stolen what was mine," Kwame spat, his voice thick with anger. "You have brought shame upon my family and dishonor to this village."

Malik stood his ground, his eyes unwavering. "Amina is not a possession to be stolen, Kwame. She is a woman with her own heart, her own mind. She chose me, just as I chose her."

"She was betrothed to me! It was her duty to marry me!" Kwame roared, his fists clenching. "You have no right to her!"

"Tradition should not dictate matters of the heart, Kwame. Love cannot be forced, nor can it be denied," Malik replied calmly, though his body was tense, ready for a fight.

Kwame lunged forward, grabbing Malik by the throat. "You will pay for this! You will pay for stealing Amina from me!"

Malik struggled against Kwame's grip, his face turning red. "Let her go, Kwame! This is between you and me!"

"This is about honor! This is about tradition! And you, Malik, have defiled both!" Kwame tightened his grip, his eyes filled with a murderous rage. "I should kill you where you stand!"

The air in the ancestral home hung thick with unspoken accusations and simmering resentment. The grand courtyard, usually a place of laughter and communal activity, was now a somber arena. Every member of Amina's extended family had gathered, their faces etched with a mixture of anger, disappointment, and a sliver of reluctant sympathy. The elders sat in a semi-circle, their weathered faces betraying the weight of tradition and the gravity of the situation. Mansa, his eyes like chips of flint, sat at the head, his presence radiating an almost palpable disapproval. Jamila, her face etched with worry lines, sat beside him, her hand resting gently on his arm, a silent plea for compassion.

The atmosphere was charged, a palpable tension that crackled in the air. The younger members of the family, Zuri and Tyrone among them, sat on the periphery, their faces a mixture of fear and curiosity. They had never witnessed such a formal gathering, a trial of sorts, where the fate of one of their own hung in the balance. Amina stood in the center of the courtyard, her head held high, but her eyes betraying a flicker of fear. Malik stood beside her, his hand gently resting on her back, a silent promise of unwavering support. He was an outsider, an unwelcome presence in this sacred space, but his love for Amina gave him the courage to stand firm.

The silence stretched, heavy and suffocating, broken only by the occasional rustle of clothing or the nervous cough of a family member. Mansa finally broke the silence, his voice raspy with age and disapproval. "We are gathered here today to decide the fate of Amina," he began, his words echoing through the courtyard. "She has brought shame upon our family, defied our traditions, and abandoned her duty. Her actions have consequences, and we must decide what those consequences will be."

The accusations flew, sharp and stinging, like poisoned darts. Aunt Fatima, her voice laced with bitterness, spoke of the dishonor Amina had brought upon the family name. Uncle Dele, his face contorted with anger, accused her of betraying their ancestors and abandoning their cultural heritage. Even some of Amina's cousins, once her closest confidantes, turned their backs on her, their faces etched with disapproval.

Jabulani, Amina's progressive uncle, stepped forward, his voice a calming balm amidst the storm of accusations. "We must remember that Amina is still one of us," he pleaded, his eyes searching the faces of his family members. "She has made a choice, yes, but we must try to understand her reasons. Love is a powerful force, and we cannot simply dismiss it."

The debate raged on, the family divided between those who demanded strict adherence to tradition and those who advocated for compassion and understanding. The younger generation, inspired by Amina's courage, began to question the rigid customs that had governed their lives for so long. Zuri, emboldened by her cousin's defiance, spoke out against the arranged marriages and the lack of freedom afforded to women in their community. Tyrone, his voice filled with passion, argued that love should be the foundation of any marriage, not family alliances or societal expectations.

Jamila, the family matriarch, finally rose to her feet, her presence commanding attention and respect. Her voice, though frail with age, carried a weight of wisdom and experience. "We must remember the values that have always guided us," she said, her eyes sweeping across the faces of her family members. "Love, compassion, and forgiveness. Amina has made a mistake, yes, but we must not abandon her. She is still our daughter, our sister, our granddaughter. We must find a way to reconcile our traditions with the realities of the modern world."

The tension in the courtyard remained palpable, but Jamila's words had planted a seed of hope, a glimmer of possibility that reconciliation might be within reach. The family members began to murmur amongst themselves, their faces reflecting a newfound sense of contemplation. The decision of whether to accept Amina back into the fold or to continue to ostracize her hung heavy in the air, a pivotal moment that would determine the future of their family and the fate of Amina's heart.

Kwame watched the proceedings with a complex mix of emotions. He had come seeking justice, perhaps even revenge, but the sight of Amina standing defiantly, yet vulnerable, stirred something within him. He saw the love in Malik's eyes, the unwavering support he offered, and a flicker of understanding ignited within his heart. He began to question his own motives, his own adherence to tradition, and the true meaning of family honor.

The weight of the decision pressed down on Mansa, the patriarch torn between his unwavering commitment to tradition and the love he held for his granddaughter. He looked at Amina, her eyes pleading for understanding, and saw a reflection of his own youthful defiance, a time when he too had challenged the expectations of his elders. He knew that whatever decision he made would have far-reaching consequences, shaping the future of his family for generations to come. The fate of Amina, and perhaps the very soul of their family, rested in his hands.

The air in the ancestral home was thick with unspoken accusations and simmering resentments. Amina's defiance had not only shattered the carefully constructed image of the family but had also exposed the fault lines that had long been hidden beneath the surface of tradition. Mansa, the patriarch, remained unyielding, his face a mask of disappointment and anger. He refused to speak Amina's name, referring to her only as "the disgraced one." His unwavering stance fueled the division, creating a chasm between those who clung to the old ways and those who dared to question them.

Jamila, the matriarch, tried to bridge the gap, her heart aching for her granddaughter. She saw the pain in Amina's eyes, the conflict between duty and desire that had driven her to make such a drastic choice. But even Jamila, with her gentle wisdom and unwavering faith, struggled to reconcile Amina's actions with the deeply ingrained beliefs of their community. She pleaded with Mansa to soften his heart, to see the love that had motivated Amina's rebellion, but her words seemed to fall on deaf ears.

The younger generation, too, was divided. Zuri, Amina's cousin, admired her courage but feared the consequences of her actions. She saw the pain and isolation that Amina now faced and wondered if the price of freedom was too high. Tyrone, on the other hand, was emboldened by Amina's defiance. He questioned the traditions that seemed to stifle individuality and limit personal choice. He saw in Amina a symbol of hope, a beacon of change in a world that desperately needed it.

Kwame, the jilted suitor, was consumed by a mixture of anger and humiliation. He had been publicly rejected, his pride wounded, his future uncertain. He struggled to understand Amina's choice, to comprehend how she could abandon the life that had been planned for her, the life that he had been so eager to share. His anger festered, fueled by the whispers and judgments of the community. He felt betrayed, not only by Amina but also by the traditions that had failed to protect him from such public disgrace.

Jabulani, Amina's progressive uncle, found himself caught in the middle. He understood Amina's desire for freedom, her yearning for a love that transcended tradition. But he also recognized the importance of family and community, the bonds that held them together. He tried to mediate between Mansa and the younger generation, to find a path that honored both the past and the future. But his efforts were often met with resistance, his words lost in the storm of emotions that raged within the family.

The once-harmonious household was now a battleground of conflicting ideologies and wounded emotions. Mealtimes were strained, conversations stilted, and the laughter that had once filled the rooms was replaced by an oppressive silence. The family, once a source of strength and support, was now fractured, each member grappling with their own doubts and fears.

Mansa, fueled by his unwavering belief in tradition, saw Amina's actions as a personal affront, a betrayal of everything he held dear. He refused to acknowledge her pain, her longing for love, her desire for a life of her own choosing. He saw only defiance, a rejection of the values that had sustained their family for generations.

Jamila, guided by her unwavering faith, saw the potential for healing and reconciliation. She believed that love could conquer all, that even the deepest wounds could be healed through forgiveness and understanding. She refused to give up on Amina, clinging to the hope that one day, the family would be whole again.

Zuri, torn between admiration and fear, struggled to reconcile her own desires with the expectations of her family. She longed for a life of her own, a life free from the constraints of tradition. But she also feared the consequences of defying her elders, of risking the love and acceptance of her community.

Kwame, consumed by anger and humiliation, sought solace in the familiar comforts of tradition. He clung to the belief that Amina had made a mistake, that she would eventually come to her senses and return to the life that had been planned for her. But deep down, he knew that things could never be the same, that Amina's actions had changed everything.

Jabulani, burdened by the weight of his family's expectations, struggled to find a way to bridge the divide. He knew that change was inevitable, that the old ways could not endure forever. But he also recognized the importance of preserving their cultural heritage, of honoring the traditions that had shaped their identity.

As the days turned into weeks, the divisions within the family deepened, threatening to tear them apart completely. The once-unbreakable bonds of kinship were now strained, stretched to the breaking point by the weight of Amina's choices. The family stood at a crossroads, uncertain of the path ahead, unsure if they could ever find their way back to each other.

The air in the ancestral home hung thick with unspoken accusations and simmering resentments. Amina's defiance had not only broken a sacred tradition but had also fractured the very foundation upon which their family stood. Each member now wrestled with their own interpretation of Amina's actions, their individual values clashing against the collective expectations that had always bound them together. Mansa, the patriarch, remained unyielding, his face a mask of disappointment and anger. He saw Amina's choice as a personal affront, a blatant disregard for his authority and the legacy he had worked so hard to preserve.

Jamila, the matriarch, though deeply saddened by the rift, couldn't entirely condemn Amina. She remembered her own youthful longings, the dreams she had once harbored before succumbing to the weight of tradition. A flicker of understanding sparked within her, a silent acknowledgment of the courage it took to defy societal norms. Yet, she also felt the sting of Amina's actions, the disruption it had caused to the family's harmony. She yearned for reconciliation, but the path seemed fraught with obstacles.

Kwame, consumed by a potent mix of heartbreak and humiliation, struggled to comprehend Amina's rejection. He had envisioned a future with her, a life built on mutual respect and shared values. Now, his dreams lay shattered, replaced by a burning desire for retribution. He saw Malik as the interloper, the outsider who had stolen what was rightfully his. His anger festered, threatening to erupt into violence.

Jabulani, ever the voice of reason, attempted to bridge the widening gap between tradition and modernity. He understood Amina's yearning for personal fulfillment, her desire to choose her own destiny. He had always encouraged her to pursue her education, to explore the world beyond their village. However, he also recognized the importance of respecting their cultural heritage, the delicate balance between honoring the past and embracing the future. He found himself caught between his loyalty to his family and his empathy for Amina's plight.

Zuri, caught in the crossfire of this familial storm, grappled with her own burgeoning desires for independence. Amina's rebellion had ignited a spark within her, a yearning to break free from the constraints of tradition. She admired Amina's courage, her willingness to defy expectations. However, she also witnessed the pain and suffering that Amina's actions had caused, the deep divisions that had emerged within their family. She wondered if the price of freedom was worth the cost.

Even the younger children in the family sensed the tension, the unspoken unease that permeated their home. They witnessed the hushed conversations, the worried expressions on their parents' faces. They didn't fully understand the complexities of the situation, but they knew that something was terribly wrong. The harmony that had once characterized their family life had been shattered, replaced by a palpable sense of discord.

The family's dynamics, once a tapestry woven with shared values and mutual respect, now resembled a battlefield, each member entrenched in their own position, unwilling to yield. The weight of tradition pressed heavily upon them, a constant reminder of the expectations they were bound to uphold. Yet, the allure of personal freedom, the desire to forge their own paths, tugged at their hearts, creating a profound sense of internal conflict.

Reconciling these conflicting values seemed an impossible task. How could they honor their heritage while also embracing the changing world around them? How could they uphold family unity while also respecting individual autonomy? These questions hung in the air, unanswered, as the family grappled with the consequences of Amina's actions.

The challenge lay not only in resolving the immediate conflict but also in redefining the very essence of their family. Could they find a way to bridge the gap between tradition and modernity, to create a new framework that honored both their past and their future? Or would they remain trapped in a cycle of resentment and division, forever haunted by the choices that had torn them apart?

As the days turned into weeks, the family remained locked in a state of uneasy truce. The silence was punctuated by occasional outbursts of anger and frustration, but also by moments of quiet reflection and introspection. Each member was forced to confront their own beliefs and values, to examine the choices they had made and the paths they had chosen. The journey towards reconciliation would be long and arduous, but it was a journey they had to undertake if they hoped to salvage what remained of their family.

The air crackled with unspoken animosity as Kwame and Malik found themselves in the same vicinity, the tension thick enough to cut with a knife. Kwame, fueled by the humiliation of Amina's rejection and the perceived theft of his future, saw Malik as the embodiment of everything wrong with the changing times – a symbol of disrespect for tradition and a threat to the established order.

Malik, on the other hand, viewed Kwame as a product of a system that stifled individual choice and perpetuated outdated customs. He saw the pain in Amina's eyes, the longing for a life beyond the confines of arranged marriage, and he couldn't stand idly by while she was forced into a life of unhappiness.

Their opposing views on tradition and love became a focal point of the family's division, a microcosm of the larger conflict between the old ways and the new. Kwame clung to the belief that marriage was a sacred union ordained by family and community, a means of preserving lineage and ensuring stability. He couldn't comprehend Amina's desire to choose her own path, to prioritize personal happiness over familial duty.

"Love is not a game, Malik," Kwame spat, his voice laced with venom. "It is a responsibility, a commitment to something larger than oneself. You have no understanding of the sacrifices required to maintain a family's honor."

Malik met Kwame's gaze with unwavering resolve. "Honor should not come at the expense of happiness, Kwame. Love should not be a prison. Amina deserves to be with someone who cherishes her, not someone who sees her as a means to an end."

Their confrontations were not always loud and explosive. Sometimes, they were subtle, veiled in polite conversation but charged with underlying hostility. A shared glance across the courtyard, a pointed remark during a family gathering – each interaction served as a reminder of the chasm that separated them.

Kwame, despite his anger, couldn't deny the genuine affection that Amina held for Malik. He saw the way her eyes lit up in his presence, the easy laughter that flowed between them. A seed of doubt began to sprout in his mind, questioning the very foundation of his beliefs.

Was tradition truly worth sacrificing happiness? Was family honor more important than individual fulfillment? These questions gnawed at him, fueling his internal turmoil and exacerbating his resentment towards Malik.

Malik, for his part, understood Kwame's pain, the sense of betrayal and loss that he must be feeling. He knew that Kwame was a good man, caught in a system that valued conformity over individuality. But he couldn't allow Kwame's hurt to justify forcing Amina into a loveless marriage.

"I don't want to be your enemy, Kwame," Malik said during one of their rare moments of truce. "I only want Amina to be happy. If you truly love her, you should want the same."

Kwame scoffed, unable to reconcile Malik's words with his actions. "Love? You speak of love as if it were a simple thing, a fleeting emotion. It is so much more than that, Malik. It is a bond that ties families together, a foundation upon which communities are built."

The conflict between Kwame and Malik served as a catalyst for change within the family, forcing them to confront their deeply held beliefs and question the very essence of their traditions. It was a battle not just for Amina's heart, but for the soul of their community, a struggle between the past and the future, between duty and desire.

As the family gathered to decide Amina's fate, the tension between Kwame and Malik reached its peak, threatening to erupt into violence. Their opposing views on tradition and love hung heavy in the air, shaping the outcome of the judgment and determining the future of their family.

CHAPTER: 12

THE TEST OF FORGIVENESS

The air in the family compound hung thick with unspoken accusations and simmering resentment. Amina stood before her grandfather, Mansa, the weight of her actions pressing down on her. Exile had changed her, hardened her in ways she hadn't anticipated. The city, with its anonymity and indifference, had stripped away the last vestiges of the sheltered girl she once was. But it had also forged within her an unshakeable resolve, a determination to be true to herself, even if it meant standing against the very foundations of her family.

She had returned not to beg forgiveness, but to seek understanding. To make them see, if only for a moment, the world through her eyes. The world where love was not a transaction, where a woman's worth was not measured by her obedience, where happiness was not a luxury to be sacrificed on the altar of tradition.

Mansa's face was a mask of disapproval, etched with the lines of years spent upholding the customs of their ancestors. His eyes, once filled with warmth and affection for her, now held a coldness that pierced her heart. The silence stretched between them, heavy and suffocating, broken only by the distant sounds of the village.

Taking a deep breath, Amina met his gaze, her voice trembling but firm. "Grandfather," she began, "I know I have caused you great pain. I know that I have defied your wishes and brought shame upon our family. But I could not live a lie. I could not marry Kwame when my heart belonged to another."

She paused, searching for the right words, the words that could penetrate the wall of tradition that surrounded him. "Is family only about obedience, about following the path that others have laid out for us? Or is it about love, about understanding, about supporting each other even when we make choices that are different from what you expect?"

The question hung in the air, a challenge to everything Mansa held dear. It was a question that had been brewing within her for years, a question that had finally erupted in the chaos of her wedding day. It was a question that could either tear her family apart or pave the way for a new understanding.

Mansa remained silent, his expression unreadable. The other family members watched with bated breath, their faces a mixture of curiosity, apprehension, and judgment. Jamila, her grandmother, offered a small, encouraging nod, but even her support couldn't ease the tension that filled the room.

Amina continued, her voice gaining strength. "I understand the importance of our traditions, Grandfather. I respect the sacrifices that our ancestors made to preserve our way of life. But times are changing. The world is changing. And we must adapt if we are to survive."

"We cannot cling to the past so tightly that we suffocate the future. We cannot force our children to live lives that are not their own. We must allow them to choose their own paths, even if those paths lead them away from what we know and understand."

She stepped closer to Mansa, her eyes pleading. "Is family built on obedience, Grandfather? Or is it built on love? Is it built on fear, or is it built on trust? Is it built on the past, or is it built on the future?"

The weight of her words settled upon the room, a challenge to the very core of their beliefs. Amina had spoken her truth, laid bare her soul. Now, all that remained was to wait for Mansa's answer, an answer that would determine not only her fate but the fate of her family as well.

The silence that followed was deafening. Every eye was on Mansa, waiting for him to speak, to pass judgment, to either condemn or forgive. Amina held her breath, her heart pounding in her chest. The future of her family, her love, her very life, hung in the balance, dependent on the words that were about to be spoken.

Amina stood before her grandfather, Mansa, the weight of generations pressing down on her. The air in the courtyard was thick with unspoken accusations, the silence broken only by the rustling of leaves in the ancient trees that had witnessed countless family dramas unfold. She had defied him, defied tradition, and in doing so, had seemingly shattered the very foundation of their family. But she knew, deep in her heart, that true strength lay not in blind obedience, but in the courage to question, to seek a path that honored both her heritage and her own soul.

"Grandfather," she began, her voice trembling slightly but firm, "is family truly built on obedience? Is love merely a transaction, a duty to be performed? Or is it the very essence of what binds us together, the invisible thread that connects our hearts across time and circumstance?"

Her words hung in the air, challenging the very core of Mansa's beliefs. He had always seen himself as the protector of tradition, the guardian of their family's honor. But Amina's rebellion had forced him to confront a truth he had long avoided: that tradition, without love and understanding, could become a cage, stifling the very spirit it was meant to nurture.

Then, a voice, unexpected and yet somehow inevitable, broke the silence. It was Malik. He stepped forward, his eyes meeting Mansa's with unwavering resolve. "Mansa," he said, his voice resonating with sincerity, "I understand your concern for tradition, for the well-being of your family. But I love Amina with a love that transcends tradition, a love that seeks only her happiness and fulfillment. I would never ask her to abandon her heritage, but I also believe that she has the right to choose her own destiny, to build a life based on love and mutual respect."

Jabulani, Amina's uncle, a man who had always straddled the line between tradition and progress, added his voice to the chorus. "Mansa, we cannot cling to the past so tightly that we suffocate the future. Amina's actions may have been unconventional, but they were born of a deep desire for authenticity, for a love that is freely given, not forced. We must be willing to adapt, to evolve, to create a new tradition that honors both our heritage and the individual spirit."

But the most surprising voice of all was Kwame's. He had been the jilted suitor, the man publicly humiliated by Amina's rejection. Yet, standing there, he spoke with a newfound understanding. "I came here seeking revenge," he confessed, his eyes filled with remorse. "I wanted to punish Amina for the pain she had caused me. But I have come to realize that true strength lies not in vengeance, but in forgiveness. Amina chose her own path, and while it caused me pain, I can now see that it was her right to do so. I offer her my forgiveness, and I hope that one day, she can forgive me for the anger I harbored."

Kwame's words were a turning point. His willingness to forgive, to acknowledge Amina's right to choose, challenged the family's long-held beliefs about honor and duty. It was a testament to the power of empathy, the ability to see the world through another's eyes, even when it meant confronting one's own prejudices and assumptions.

Malik's intervention was crucial, not just as Amina's lover, but as a man who, despite being an outsider, understood the importance of family and community. He wasn't advocating for a complete abandonment of tradition, but rather for a reinterpretation, a way to integrate modern values with ancestral customs.

Jabulani's progressive stance, often whispered in private, now found a voice in the open. He represented the changing tides, the younger generation's yearning for a world where tradition and personal freedom could coexist. His words were a plea for understanding, a bridge between the old and the new.

And Kwame, the man scorned, his voice cracking with newfound humility, offered the most profound challenge of all. His forgiveness wasn't just a personal act; it was a dismantling of the very foundation of vengeance that often fueled their traditions. It was a radical act of love, a testament to the transformative power of understanding.

These voices, each representing a different facet of their complex family dynamic, echoed through the courtyard, challenging Mansa to reconsider his rigid adherence to tradition. They spoke of love, forgiveness, and the importance of individual choice, concepts that had long been overshadowed by the weight of duty and expectation. The seeds of doubt had been planted, and Mansa, for the first time in his life, found himself questioning the very principles he had always held dear.

The weight of his decision pressed heavily upon him. He looked at Amina, her eyes filled with a mixture of hope and trepidation. He saw not a rebellious daughter, but a woman of courage and conviction, a woman who was willing to risk everything for the sake of love and authenticity. And in that moment, he began to understand that true honor lay not in upholding tradition at all costs, but in embracing the ever-evolving nature of the human heart.

Amina stood before her family, the weight of their judgment pressing down on her like the heavy robes she had once been expected to wear on her wedding day. The air in the ancestral home was thick with unspoken accusations, the silence punctuated only by the crackling fire in the hearth, a fire that seemed to mirror the turmoil raging within her.

She had defied tradition, broken a sacred vow, and brought shame upon her family. But as she looked into the faces of her elders, she saw not only anger but also a flicker of something else—perhaps confusion, perhaps even a hint of understanding. It was this glimmer of hope that fueled her plea.

"Grandfather," she began, her voice trembling slightly but gaining strength with each word, "I know I have caused you great pain. I never intended to dishonor our family, but I could not live a lie. I could not marry Kwame when my heart belonged to another."

She paused, her gaze sweeping across the room, meeting the eyes of her mother, her aunts, her uncles. "Is family truly built on obedience alone? Is there no room for love, for happiness, for the choices that make us who we are?"

Amina stepped forward, her hands outstretched in a gesture of supplication. "I understand the importance of our traditions, the bonds that tie us together. But traditions must also evolve, must adapt to the changing times. Can we not find a way to honor our past while embracing our future?"

Her eyes met Kwame's, and she saw a flicker of pain in his usually stoic expression. "Kwame," she said softly, "I am sorry for the hurt I have caused you. You are a good man, and you deserve to be loved fully and completely. I could not give you that, and it would have been a disservice to both of us to pretend otherwise."

Turning back to Mansa, she continued, "I am not asking you to abandon our traditions, Grandfather. I am simply asking you to open your heart to the possibility that there is more than one path to happiness. That love can be found outside the confines of arranged marriages, that a woman can choose her own destiny without betraying her family."

She spoke of the love she shared with Malik, not as a defiance of their customs, but as a testament to the power of connection, of finding a soulmate in a world often dictated by practicality and obligation. She painted a picture of a future where tradition and personal choice could coexist, where families could support individual happiness without sacrificing their values.

"I know it will take time for you to understand," she said, her voice filled with emotion. "But I beg you, do not let anger and pride blind you to the possibility of forgiveness. Do not let tradition become a prison that keeps us from loving and supporting one another."

Amina's words hung in the air, a challenge to the very foundation of their beliefs. The silence that followed was heavy, pregnant with the weight of generations, the echoes of countless decisions made in the name of duty and tradition. Would her plea be heard? Would her family find it in their hearts to forgive her, to understand her, to embrace a future where love and tradition could coexist?

The fire crackled again, a small spark leaping from the hearth, as if mirroring the hope that flickered within Amina's heart. She had spoken her truth, laid bare her soul, and now all she could do was wait, praying that her family would choose love over tradition, forgiveness over condemnation, and a future where she could once again be a part of their lives.

The fate of her family, and perhaps the future of their traditions, hung in the balance, suspended between the weight of the past and the promise of a new beginning. Amina's plea was not just for herself, but for all those who dared to dream of a world where love could conquer all, even the most deeply entrenched customs.

The air in the courtyard hung thick with unspoken words, each breath a testament to the chasm that had grown between Amina and her family. The accusations, the hurt, the raw sting of betrayal—it all lingered, a palpable barrier against any hope of reconciliation. But amidst the tension, a flicker of something else began to stir: the possibility, however faint, of forgiveness.

Amina's plea, raw and heartfelt, had planted a seed. Could they, as a family, truly condemn her for following her heart? Was tradition so rigid that it allowed no room for love, for individual choice? The questions hung in the air, unanswered, as each member of the family wrestled with their own convictions.

Jamila, the family matriarch, stepped forward, her voice a soothing balm against the harshness of the preceding exchanges. "We are a family," she reminded them, her eyes sweeping across the faces of her children and grandchildren. "And what is a family without forgiveness? Without the willingness to mend what is broken?"

Her words resonated, a gentle nudge towards the path of healing. But Mansa remained unmoved, his face a mask of stubborn pride. "She has shamed us," he declared, his voice unwavering. "Tradition has been broken. There must be consequences."

But even in his unwavering stance, a subtle shift was perceptible. The fire in his eyes had dimmed, replaced by a flicker of doubt. He saw the pain in Amina's eyes, the genuine remorse for the hurt she had caused. And he knew, deep down, that forgiveness was not a sign of weakness, but of strength.

Jabulani, ever the voice of reason, added his perspective. "We cannot cling to the past so tightly that we suffocate the future," he argued. "Amina has made her choice, and while it may not align with our traditions, we must respect her courage to follow her heart."

Even Kwame, the jilted groom, found himself grappling with unexpected emotions. The anger and humiliation still burned, but beneath the surface, a grudging respect for Amina's conviction began to emerge. He had come seeking retribution, but now, faced with the possibility of forgiveness, he found himself questioning his own motives.

"I came here seeking justice," Kwame admitted, his voice laced with a hint of vulnerability. "But perhaps... perhaps what we all need is not justice, but healing." His words hung in the air, a testament to the transformative power of forgiveness.

Amina watched, her heart swelling with a mixture of hope and trepidation. Could they truly forgive her? Could they accept her choice and embrace her, despite the pain she had caused? The answer, she knew, lay not in her words, but in their hearts.

The silence stretched, heavy and pregnant with anticipation. Then, slowly, deliberately, Mansa stepped forward. His face was etched with a lifetime of tradition, but his eyes held a glimmer of something new: understanding.

"Forgiveness," he said, his voice raspy with emotion, "is not forgetting. It is choosing to see beyond the hurt, to embrace the possibility of healing." He extended his hand towards Amina, a gesture of reconciliation, of acceptance.

Tears streamed down Amina's face as she reached out and clasped her grandfather's hand. The chasm that had separated them began to close, replaced by a fragile bridge of forgiveness. The journey to healing would be long and arduous, but in that moment, a new chapter had begun—a chapter defined not by tradition alone, but by the transformative power of love and forgiveness.

The scene served as a potent reminder that even the deepest wounds can be healed, that even the most entrenched beliefs can be challenged, and that forgiveness, though difficult, is always possible. It was a testament to the resilience of the human spirit and the enduring power of love to overcome even the most formidable obstacles. The path forward was still uncertain, but with forgiveness as their guide, the family could begin to rebuild, to redefine their traditions, and to create a future where love and duty could coexist in harmony.

The air in the ancestral home hung thick with unspoken tension. Amina's plea had landed like a stone in a still pond, the ripples of her question – "Is family built on obedience or love?" – spreading through the hearts of everyone present. The silence that followed was heavy, each member of the family grappling with the implications of her words. Mansa, the patriarch, sat rigid on his stool, his face a mask of disapproval. Jamila, the matriarch, watched with a glimmer of hope in her eyes, her heart aching for the fractured bonds of her family.

The seeds of doubt had been sown. Malik's heartfelt declaration of his love for Amina, Jabulani's quiet but firm support of her right to choose, and even Kwame's unexpected admission of his own internal conflict had created cracks in the seemingly impenetrable wall of tradition. But cracks were not enough; a bridge needed to be built, a common ground discovered where tradition and personal freedom could coexist.

Reconciliation was not about abandoning tradition entirely, but about re-evaluating its place in a changing world. It was about understanding that love, compassion, and individual happiness were not threats to family honor, but rather, essential components of a thriving community. The path to reconciliation was fraught with challenges, requiring humility, empathy, and a willingness to compromise.

Amina, despite the pain of her exile and the sting of her family's rejection, knew that she had to be the one to extend the olive branch. She had to show them that her love for Malik did not diminish her love for her family, that her desire for personal freedom did not equate to disrespect for her heritage. She had to prove that it was possible to honor the past while embracing the future.

She began by acknowledging the pain she had caused, expressing her regret for the public humiliation she had inflicted on her family, particularly Mansa. She explained that her actions were not intended to defy tradition, but to affirm her right to choose her own path, a right she believed was inherent in her faith and her humanity. She spoke of the importance of love in marriage, arguing that a union built on coercion and obligation could never truly bring happiness or strengthen family bonds.

Her words were met with a mixture of skepticism and grudging admiration. Some family members remained steadfast in their adherence to tradition, viewing Amina's actions as a betrayal of their values. Others, particularly the younger generation, were more open to her perspective, recognizing the validity of her desire for personal autonomy.

Jamila, the matriarch, stepped forward, her voice filled with wisdom and compassion. She reminded the family of the importance of forgiveness, of the need to heal the wounds that had been inflicted by anger and resentment. She spoke of the strength of family bonds, arguing that love and understanding were more powerful than rigid adherence to tradition.

Kwame, surprisingly, also offered a perspective that leaned towards reconciliation. He admitted that while he had initially been consumed by anger and a desire for revenge, he had come to realize that forcing someone to love you was not true love at all. He acknowledged Amina's courage in choosing her own path, even if it meant defying tradition.

The turning point came when Mansa, the patriarch, finally spoke. His voice was low and gravelly, filled with a lifetime of upholding tradition and protecting his family's honor. He admitted that he had been blinded by his own beliefs, unable to see the pain he had inflicted on Amina. He acknowledged that love, not obedience, should be the foundation of a family.

Mansa's words were a watershed moment, signaling a shift in the family's perspective. He extended his hand to Amina, a gesture of forgiveness and acceptance. Amina, tears streaming down her face, grasped his hand, the physical connection symbolizing the mending of their broken bond. The path to reconciliation was not complete, but a significant step had been taken.

The importance of finding common ground became clear. It wasn't about one side winning and the other losing, but about creating a space where tradition and personal choice could coexist. It was about finding a balance between honoring the past and embracing the future, about recognizing that family honor could be upheld through love, compassion, and understanding, rather than through rigid adherence to outdated customs.

The process of reconciliation would be ongoing, requiring constant communication, empathy, and a willingness to compromise. But the seeds of healing had been sown, and the family, though still scarred by the events of the past, was now united in its commitment to building a future where love and tradition could thrive together. The journey towards finding common ground had begun, promising a future where faith and fire could forge a new path, one built on understanding, forgiveness, and the enduring power of love.

CHAPTER: 13

REDEMPTION & NEW BEGINNINGS

The air in the village was thick with anticipation. The elders, the family, even Kwame, sat in a circle, the weight of their decision heavy on their faces. Amina stood before them, Malik by her side, their hands clasped together, a silent testament to their unwavering love. The past weeks had been a whirlwind of emotions – anger, resentment, forgiveness, and finally, a glimmer of understanding. Jamila, the matriarch, had been instrumental in calming the storm, her wisdom and compassion guiding the family towards a resolution.

Mansa, the patriarch, his face etched with years of tradition, finally spoke, his voice raspy but firm. "We have listened to the pleas, the arguments, the cries of our hearts. Tradition is the bedrock of our community, but love, true love, is a gift from God. To deny it is to deny His grace."

He paused, his gaze sweeping over Amina and Malik. "We cannot erase the past, nor can we ignore the customs that have shaped us. But we can find a new path, one that honors our heritage while embracing the future."

The decision was a compromise, a delicate dance between the old and the new. Amina and Malik would be allowed to marry, but with conditions. Malik would have to undergo a period of initiation, learning the ways of the village, proving his commitment to the community. He would have to contribute to the village, not just as an individual, but as a member of the family.

Amina would also have a role to play. She would become a bridge between the generations, teaching the younger ones about the importance of tradition while also encouraging them to embrace their own dreams and aspirations. She would be a symbol of change, a reminder that progress and heritage could coexist.

Kwame, surprisingly, was the first to offer his congratulations. His heart was still wounded, but he recognized the depth of Amina's love for Malik. He understood that forcing her into a loveless marriage would have been a greater tragedy. He extended his hand to Malik, a gesture of acceptance and forgiveness.

"I wish you both happiness," he said, his voice sincere. "May your love bring strength and unity to our community."

The village erupted in cheers, a collective sigh of relief washing over them. The tension that had gripped them for so long finally dissipated, replaced by a sense of hope and renewal. The decision was not perfect, but it was a step forward, a testament to their ability to adapt and evolve.

Amina and Malik embraced, their hearts overflowing with gratitude. They knew that their journey was far from over, but they were ready to face whatever challenges lay ahead, together. They had proven that love could conquer all, even the most deeply entrenched traditions.

As the sun set over the village, casting a golden glow on the faces of the gathered community, Amina knew that she had made the right choice. She had honored her family, stayed true to her faith, and followed her heart. She had found a way to reconcile tradition and modernity, paving the way for a brighter future for herself and her loved ones. The fire of her faith had met the fire of her love, and together, they had forged a new path, a path of redemption and new beginnings.

The air in the village square crackled with a newfound energy, a blend of respect for the past and a hesitant embrace of the future. The elders, after days of deliberation and soul-searching, had reached a decision that resonated with both tradition and the undeniable truth of Amina's heart. It was a compromise, a delicate balance that allowed Amina to pursue her love for Malik while still honoring her family's legacy.

Amina stood before her family, her heart pounding with anticipation. Mansa, his face etched with a mixture of pride and resignation, addressed the crowd. He spoke of the importance of tradition, of the bonds that held their community together, but also of the need to recognize the changing times and the power of love. He announced that Amina would not be forced into a marriage against her will, but that she would also be expected to uphold the values of their family and community.

The terms of the agreement were carefully laid out. Amina and Malik would be allowed to marry, but they would also be required to contribute to the community in a meaningful way. They would work together to establish a school that would teach both traditional values and modern skills, ensuring that future generations would be equipped to navigate the complexities of the world while still honoring their heritage.

Amina's eyes welled up with tears as she listened to Mansa's words. It was more than she could have ever hoped for. She had expected to be exiled, to be cut off from her family and community forever. But instead, she was being offered a chance to bridge the gap between her love for Malik and her loyalty to her family.

Malik, standing beside her, squeezed her hand reassuringly. He had been prepared to fight for Amina, to defy tradition and risk everything for their love. But he also understood the importance of family and community, and he was grateful for the opportunity to prove himself worthy in the eyes of Amina's family.

The wedding that followed was unlike any the village had ever seen. It was a celebration of love, of tradition, and of the power of forgiveness. Amina wore a traditional wedding gown, but she also incorporated elements that reflected her own personality and her love for Malik. The ceremony was a blend of ancient rituals and modern expressions of love, a symbol of the new era that was dawning in the village.

As Amina and Malik exchanged vows, they looked into each other's eyes and saw a future filled with hope and promise. They knew that their journey would not be easy, that they would face challenges and obstacles along the way. But they also knew that they had the love and support of their family and community, and that together, they could overcome anything.

The establishment of the school became Amina and Malik's shared passion. They poured their hearts and souls into creating a place where children could learn, grow, and discover their own potential. Amina taught the children about their cultural heritage, about the importance of family and community, and about the power of faith. Malik taught them practical skills that would help them succeed in the modern world, such as computer literacy and entrepreneurship.

The school quickly became a beacon of hope in the village, attracting students from all walks of life. It was a place where tradition and modernity could coexist, where children could learn to honor their past while also embracing the future. Amina and Malik's vision was slowly but surely transforming the village, creating a community that was both rooted in its heritage and open to new possibilities.

Even Kwame, initially consumed by anger and resentment, found a path to healing and forgiveness. He witnessed Amina and Malik's dedication to the community and recognized the genuine love that they shared. He eventually became a supporter of the school, contributing his own skills and resources to help it thrive. In time, he even found love again, marrying a woman who shared his passion for preserving their cultural heritage.

Zuri, inspired by Amina's courage, continued to challenge the traditional norms in her own way. She excelled in her studies and became a role model for other young women in the village. She used her voice to advocate for gender equality and to empower women to pursue their dreams. She never forgot the lessons she had learned from Amina, and she carried her spirit of rebellion and determination with her wherever she went.

The village, once divided by tradition and conflict, began to heal and unite. The elders recognized the wisdom of Amina's choices and embraced the changes that were taking place. They realized that tradition was not about clinging to the past, but about adapting to the present while still honoring the values that had sustained them for generations.

Amina's journey had not been easy, but it had been worth it. She had found a way to honor her family while also pursuing her own happiness. She had shown her community that love and tradition could coexist, that it was possible to embrace the future without abandoning the past. And in doing so, she had paved the way for a brighter future for herself, for her family, and for her entire village.

The air crackled with a newfound energy as Mansa, his voice softened yet firm, declared his decision. Amina would not be forced into a marriage against her will. Kwame, though initially stung by the rejection, had witnessed the depth of Amina's love for Malik and the unwavering support she received from Jabulani and even Jamila. He, too, had begun to question the rigidity of tradition, realizing that true honor lay not in blind obedience, but in understanding and compassion.

Amina, tears streaming down her face, rushed to embrace her grandfather. The years of tradition, the weight of expectation, seemed to lift from her shoulders in that single moment. Malik, standing beside her, felt a surge of gratitude towards Mansa, a man he had once perceived as an unyielding obstacle. He understood now that Mansa's actions stemmed from a deep-seated desire to protect his family and uphold their values, not from malice or cruelty.

The resolution was not without compromise. Amina and Malik would remain in the village, contributing to its growth and prosperity. They would, however, be allowed to marry according to their own wishes, with the blessing of the family. Kwame, displaying remarkable grace, offered his friendship to both Amina and Malik, acknowledging that their love was genuine and deserving of respect. He would, in time, find his own path to happiness, perhaps even challenging tradition in his own way.

The wedding that followed was unlike any the village had ever seen. It was a celebration of love, faith, and the delicate balance between tradition and modernity. Amina, radiant in a gown that blended traditional fabrics with contemporary design, walked down the aisle towards Malik, her heart overflowing with joy. The ceremony incorporated both Christian and traditional elements, symbolizing the harmonious coexistence of faith and culture.

As Amina and Malik embarked on their married life, they became beacons of hope for the younger generation. Zuri, inspired by Amina's courage, resolved to pursue her education and challenge the limitations placed upon women in the village. Tyrone, witnessing the transformative power of forgiveness, began to mend his relationship with his own family, understanding that true strength lay in reconciliation, not rebellion.

The story, however, does not end with a simple happily ever after. The seeds of change had been sown, but the path ahead was not without its thorns. The older generation, while accepting of Amina's choices, still clung to many of their traditional beliefs. The delicate balance achieved was fragile, requiring constant effort and understanding to maintain.

Rumors began to circulate about Tumelo, a distant relative who had been living in the city. He was said to be ambitious and ruthless, with a desire to claim his place within the family hierarchy. His arrival in the village threatened to disrupt the newfound harmony and reignite old conflicts. What were his true intentions? Was he a force for progress or a harbinger of chaos?

Kwame, still grappling with his own heartbreak, found himself drawn to Tumelo's charisma and ambition. Could Tumelo offer him a way to regain his lost status and exact revenge on Amina and Malik? Or would Kwame rise above his bitterness and choose a path of forgiveness and reconciliation?

Amina and Malik, aware of the looming challenges, vowed to protect their love and the newfound peace within their family. They understood that the battle for acceptance and understanding was far from over. They would need to rely on their faith, their love for each other, and the unwavering support of their allies to navigate the treacherous waters ahead.

And so, the first chapter of Amina's story comes to a close, leaving readers with a sense of hope and anticipation. The themes of tradition versus modernity, faith versus doubt, and love versus duty will continue to be explored in Book 2, as Amina and her family face new challenges and strive to create a brighter future for themselves and their community. The journey has just begun, and the stakes are higher than ever.

The question of Tumelo's true identity and intentions hangs heavy in the air, promising a turbulent future. Will he become a catalyst for positive change, or will he tear the family apart? The answer lies in the choices that Amina, Malik, Kwame, and the other members of their community will make in the face of adversity.

The ending serves as a powerful reminder that even in the face of seemingly insurmountable obstacles, love, faith, and forgiveness can triumph. But it also cautions that the fight for progress is never truly over, and that vigilance and understanding are essential to maintaining the delicate balance between tradition and modernity. The stage is set for a new chapter, filled with intrigue, drama, and the enduring power of the human spirit.

The air in the village hung thick with the scent of reconciliation, a stark contrast to the bitterness that had permeated it just weeks before. Amina, standing beside Malik, felt the weight of her family's gaze, a mixture of acceptance and lingering apprehension. The final decision, brokered by Jamila's unwavering faith and Jabulani's progressive vision, allowed Amina to marry Malik, but with a condition: they would remain in the village, contributing to its well-being and respecting its traditions.

This wasn't the complete freedom Amina had initially craved, the escape from the constraints of her upbringing. Yet, it was a compromise, a bridge between two worlds. She realized that true strength wasn't about severing ties with the past, but about weaving it into the fabric of the future. Malik, ever supportive, understood her internal conflict. He knew Amina's heart was deeply rooted in this land, in the people who had shaped her, even those who had tried to dictate her destiny.

The wedding, a smaller, more intimate affair than the one initially planned with Kwame, was a symbol of this new understanding. Kwame, though still nursing a broken heart, offered a gesture of goodwill, a silent acknowledgment of Amina's courage and Malik's unwavering love. It was a moment of profound healing, a testament to the possibility of forgiveness and the potential for growth, even in the face of deep-seated pain.

Amina and Malik began their life together, not as rebels exiled from their home, but as active members of a community slowly embracing change. Amina started a small school, teaching the children both traditional customs and modern ideas, fostering a spirit of critical thinking and open-mindedness. Malik, with his entrepreneurial spirit, helped local farmers adopt sustainable practices, increasing their yields and improving their livelihoods.

Their presence served as a constant reminder that tradition and modernity weren't mutually exclusive. The village elders, initially skeptical, began to see the positive impact of their efforts. They witnessed the children thriving under Amina's guidance, learning to respect their heritage while also embracing new possibilities. They saw the farmers prospering, their families secure and their futures brighter.

Even Mansa, the family patriarch, softened his stance. He observed Amina's dedication to the community, her unwavering commitment to her family, and her deep-seated faith. He realized that love, not obedience, was the true foundation of a strong family. He finally offered Amina and Malik his blessing, a gesture that brought tears to Jamila's eyes and a sense of profound peace to Amina's heart.

However, the path to complete harmony wasn't without its challenges. Zuri, inspired by Amina's defiance, began to push the boundaries even further, experimenting with city life and facing the harsh realities of a world far removed from the sheltered village. Tyrone, grappling with his own identity and the expectations placed upon him, struggled to find his place in a society undergoing rapid transformation.

Amina and Malik found themselves navigating these new complexities, offering guidance and support to the younger generation, reminding them that true freedom came with responsibility and that change required careful consideration. They encouraged Zuri to find her own path but also cautioned her against reckless choices. They helped Tyrone embrace his heritage while also pursuing his dreams, showing him that he could be both a traditional man and a modern individual.

The balance between tradition and modernity became a central theme, not just in Amina's life, but in the life of the entire village. It was a delicate dance, a constant negotiation between honoring the past and embracing the future.

It required open communication, mutual respect, and a willingness to compromise.

Amina's journey, from a young woman trapped by tradition to a leader forging a new path, served as an inspiration to many. She demonstrated that it was possible to challenge the status quo without abandoning one's roots, to embrace change without losing one's identity. She showed that true strength lay not in blind obedience, but in the courage to question, to learn, and to grow.

The final scene of the book depicts Amina and Malik standing on a hill overlooking the village, their hands intertwined. The sun sets, casting a warm glow over the valley, symbolizing the hope and promise of a new beginning. The challenges ahead were undeniable, but they faced them together, united by their love, their faith, and their unwavering commitment to building a better future for themselves and for their community.

As Amina gazed at the horizon, she knew that the story of faith and fire was far from over. The embers of tradition still smoldered, and the winds of change continued to blow. But she also knew that the bonds of family, the power of love, and the resilience of the human spirit would guide them through whatever lay ahead. The journey had just begun, and she was ready to face it, hand in hand with the man she loved, in a village slowly but surely finding its balance between the old and the new.

The air in the village, once thick with tension and the scent of impending doom, now carried a whisper of hope. Amina's courageous stand had not only reshaped her own destiny but had also planted seeds of change within the very heart of the community. The elders, initially resistant to her defiance, had witnessed the power of love and the unwavering strength of a woman who dared to challenge tradition. Mansa, the patriarch, though still bearing the weight of his initial anger, had begun to see the possibility of a future where tradition and personal happiness could coexist.

The resolution, though not without its scars, had paved the way for new beginnings. Amina and Malik, hand in hand, stood as symbols of this nascent era. Their love, once a forbidden flame, now flickered as a beacon, illuminating the path for others who yearned to break free from the shackles of outdated customs. The younger generation, inspired by Amina's bravery, dared to dream of a world where their voices would be heard, and their choices respected.

Zuri, Amina's younger cousin, once caught in the web of societal expectations, now felt a newfound sense of liberation. The pressure to conform, though still present, no longer held the same suffocating grip. She began to explore her own passions, her own dreams, with a confidence that had been previously suppressed. Tyrone, too, found himself questioning the rigid norms that had defined his life. He saw in Amina's struggle a reflection of his own yearning for authenticity and self-expression.

Kwame, initially consumed by heartbreak and a thirst for revenge, had embarked on his own journey of self-discovery. The rejection had forced him to confront his own beliefs, his own values. He began to understand that true strength lay not in clinging to tradition but in embracing change and fostering understanding. He started a community project aimed at educating young men about the importance of respecting women's choices and promoting gender equality.

The village, once divided by conflicting ideologies, began to heal. The wounds of betrayal and anger slowly began to mend, replaced by a fragile yet resilient sense of unity. The church, a pillar of faith and tradition, played a crucial role in this reconciliation. Pastor Samuel, a man of wisdom and compassion, preached about the importance of forgiveness and the transformative power of love. He emphasized that faith should not be used as a weapon to enforce conformity but as a guiding light to illuminate the path towards understanding and acceptance.

Amina and Malik, though having faced immense challenges, were now ready to embrace their future together. They envisioned a life where they could honor their heritage while also forging their own path. They planned to build a home on the outskirts of the village, a place where tradition and modernity could harmoniously blend. They dreamed of raising a family rooted in love, respect, and a deep appreciation for both their cultural heritage and the boundless possibilities of the future.

The scars of the past, however, were not easily erased. The memory of the conflict, the pain of betrayal, lingered like a shadow. But Amina and Malik were determined to move forward, to build a future free from the constraints of the past. They knew that the road ahead would not be easy, but they were confident that their love, their faith, and their unwavering commitment to each other would guide them through any challenges that might arise.

The final scene depicts Amina and Malik standing on a hill overlooking the village, hand in hand, gazing towards the horizon. The sun sets, painting the sky in hues of orange and gold, symbolizing the dawn of a new era. Amina turns to Malik, her eyes filled with hope and determination. "The journey has been long and arduous," she says, "but we have emerged stronger, wiser, and more deeply in love than ever before."

Malik smiles, his eyes reflecting the same unwavering commitment. "The future is uncertain," he replies, "but we will face it together, hand in hand, with faith in our hearts and love as our guiding light." They embrace, their silhouettes outlined against the vibrant sky, a symbol of the enduring power of love and the promise of a brighter future.

The book concludes with a sense of hope and optimism, leaving the reader with the belief that even in the face of seemingly insurmountable challenges, love, faith, and the courage to challenge tradition can pave the way for new beginnings. The seeds of change have been sown, and the future of the village, though uncertain, holds the promise of a more inclusive, compassionate, and harmonious society. The stage is set for Book 2, hinting at the future challenges and triumphs that await Amina, Malik, and the evolving community.

When Faith Meets Fire: *Blood Ties & Broken Vows, A Family Saga of Forbidden Love and Tradition.* In a world where tradition reigns supreme, love is a dangerous rebellion.

Amina has spent her life straddling two worlds—one defined by ancestral customs and family honor, the other shaped by her own dreams and desires. When her family arranges her marriage to Kwame, a powerful suitor with deep ties to their community, she knows what is expected of her: obedience, sacrifice, and duty. But her heart belongs to Malik—the one man she can never have.

Malik is everything Amina's family rejects—an outsider, a self-made man, and a challenger to the rigid traditions that dictate who she should marry. Their love is intense, undeniable, and forbidden, and when it is exposed, it threatens to shatter the foundation of Amina's family.

Caught in a storm of family loyalty, cultural expectations, and faith, Amina must make an impossible choice—submit to a life chosen for her or risk everything for love. As tensions rise and secrets unravel, she faces exile, betrayal, and heartbreak, forcing her to question:

Can love survive when it is forbidden by tradition? Is faith strong enough to challenge generations of unyielding customs? How far will a family go to protect its honor—even if it means sacrificing one of their own?
A Story of Faith, Love, and the Battle for Freedom Set against a backdrop of ancestral duty, faith-driven dilemmas, and generational conflict, *When Faith Meets Fire: Blood Ties & Broken Vows* is a breathtaking and emotionally charged family saga about the price of love, the weight of tradition, and the unbreakable bonds that define us.

As the battle between love and loyalty, faith and fire, tradition and transformation rages on, one question remains:

When everything is at stake, will Amina fight for her heart—or will she let her fate be decided for her?

A deeply moving, thought-provoking novel that will keep readers on the edge of their seats, questioning the fine line between honoring the past and claiming the future

Made in the USA
Columbia, SC
27 March 2025